Now Legwarmers

Pascal O'Loughlin

CW00394546

"I wanted to reach into the book and at eventually everything

v.

tion of small town life is gly perfect, his attention xquisite.

a book."

—...n Keyes

was born in Dublin, moved to London in the 1980s, and became a Librarian at the National Poetry Library.

He won the Chroma Queer Short Story Competition in 2006, judged by Ali Smith and Michael Arditti.

His published poems, stories, zines and pamphlets include Walking Naked, Chocolochismo, RWF/RAF (*with Sarah Crewe*) and YUKIKO.

This is his debut novel.

Now Legwarmers

Pascal O'Loughlin

HENNINGHAM
FAMILY
PRESS

First published in 2018 by Henningham Family Press.
130 Sandringham Road, London, E8 2HJ
henninghamfamilypress.co.uk
@HenninghamPress

Printed and bound by T.J. International Ltd, Padstow
& Henningham Family Press, London

ISBN   9781999797416
EPUB   9781999797454
ARTISTS' BOOK (henninghamfamilypress.co.uk)

Now Legwarmers

Family badge of sapphire
and cracked emerald -
Any day now -

David Bowie - Future Legend

In memory of my parents,
Joan and Ted O'Loughlin

The road was shiny black under the orange lights. Cars whizzed up it.

'Go in that way,' she said.

She took my hand and led us off the road. I could smell tar. The ground was bumpy and I tripped in the dark but I didn't fall. We started giggling and I felt less nervous.

'Where are the others?'

I realised the question wasn't right as soon as it came out.

She let go of my hand.

'Never mind the others.'

There was no path now and the bushes were thick. We were right at the back of the estate, in the middle of nowhere really.

'Here.'

We'd come to a sort of clearing, just grass and muck and the black bits from a fire and broken bottles. There was a tree lying down. She seemed to know where we were. I'd never been here before.

She turned to face me. I knew that this was something important. I knew that the girl was doing it to the boy and that wasn't the way it usually went but it wasn't my problem.

'Come here.'

She spat her chewing gum on the ground so I spat mine too. She put her lips on my lips and opened her mouth. I did the same. She actually put her tongue inside my mouth and squirmed it around. I did the same with my tongue. It tasted minty. Her eyes were closed. We had our arms around each other. I could hear cars. It felt like an experiment. Her mouth was a cave with a seal or an otter in it. Mine must have been the same for her. The otter and the seal moved around. Her back was a birdcage under a tablecloth.

I was wondering when it would stop but then she moved her face away. Her hand went down my front to my trouser zip. Nobody ever had touched me where she put her hand. I pushed her away. I didn't want her to. It was no big deal.

Then she was taking off her jumper. She had a girl's vest underneath. She took that off. I'd never seen a girl so close-up before. Her nipples stuck out and her skin was darker than I expected. Her breasts were smaller than the ones in newspapers and magazines. She took my hands and put them there.

I didn't want to keep doing what we were doing.

'It's cold,' I said. 'You should put your vest back on.'

I took my hands away.

'Do you not like it?'

'I keep thinking the others are going to come.'

'Never mind the others,' she said, but she reached down and picked up her vest. She pulled it back over her head and then the same with her jumper.

She offered me a cigarette.

'What's your name?'

'John,' I said. Her name was Angela. We sat on the tree trunk, smoking.

'The disco was good,' she said.

'It was ok.'

'Have you just moved here?' She blew a smoke ring.

I said yes although we'd actually moved at the beginning of the summer. Then I tried to blow a smoke ring but it didn't work and she laughed.

'I like it here.' She put her arm through mine. 'Look at all the stars.'

I looked up. The sky was packed full of them. It was navy blue with millions of tiny lights. You couldn't see the moon. One airplane was making its way across the world right above us and we were sitting down here looking up. It felt special in a way that was new to me. It felt like there was nobody else in the world except us. I'd never done a lot of things before and tonight was one of them.

A scream came from somewhere behind us, then laughing.

'Sshhh. That must be them now.'

'Who?'

'The others.'

We both started laughing, but quietly so we wouldn't be heard, but that just made it worse, so we broke our hearts.

In the middle of all the laughing she started kissing me. I didn't want to push her away again and, anyway, I did really like her so I let it happen but I didn't feel anything like I read about in books. She seemed to enjoy it though so, in a way, I did too. We did all the moves but I stopped her from taking off her jumper and I didn't want to take my jumper off at all.

'What age are you?'

I said I was nearly fourteen.

'I'm nearly fifteen,' she said. 'My last boyfriend was sixteen. He tried to rape me.'

I kissed her then and it felt real. I put my tongue right in. It felt like all I wanted was for her to never be raped again.

She moved away.

'Let's have another cigarette,' she said.

I said I didn't want one but she said she definitely did, that she loved smoking.

The wind kept blowing out the matches. The others must have seen the little flames or something because they turned up out of nowhere. I didn't want either of them here even though she knew them. Their names were Pauline and Paul. I'd seen them around before, but separately, and we'd never actually spoken to each other before tonight. He looked rough, like something really bad had happened to him.

'How's she cutting?' He'd asked me the same question twice, earlier. I wasn't sure what it meant but it was about being with girls and getting off with them.

'Fine. She's cutting fine.' My voice was different to his. I pretended to laugh as if I got the joke.

'Oh Jesus.' He made his eyes go up and around, as if I'd said something stupid. It was like my answer was right but I was wrong. I could see that we were on different sides.

'You're a gas man.'

'Are you new around here?' the girl asked. She looked like an old lady with a pageboy haircut.

'I'm only after moving here,' I said.

She turned her head and spat on the ground, then she

turned back.

'What team do you follow?'

'I don't follow a team,' I said.

Angela stood up at this point and announced that we were going.

'Where?' said Paul.

'None of your business.'

Paul and Pauline looked at each other. Pauline blew a big, pink bubble. It burst and stuck to her lips but she didn't try and get it off.

'Come on,' said Angela.

I got up and followed. I turned back to look for a second. Paul was eating the bubblegum right off Pauline's face.

Then it was just the two of us walking on in the quiet. I didn't know where we were going. It was just fields.

'I need to stop for a piss,' said Angela

I needed one too so we headed for some bushes. She looked small sitting on her hunkers. I liked the sound of it coming out of us and landing on the ground.

'I hate the way people never go to the toilet in books or in films,' she said. 'When I write a book or make a film, people are going to go to the toilet.'

She pulled her pants up.

'That was him,' she said.

'Who?'

'The one who raped me. Paul. I can't believe Pauline is

with him after what he did.'

I said nothing. Everything was unusual about tonight. I didn't know what to say.

'His family rob houses, and he cut a horse's head off. And he puts bangers in snakes' mouths so their heads explode.'

'Where does he get the snakes?'

'I don't know.'

I'd never actually met anybody who'd been raped before. Meeting somebody who'd been raped and then the person who'd done the raping on the same night was doubly unusual.

We were back on the main road now, looking down on the estate. The lights of Clonduff made a flat, sparkly rectangle in the fields under the sky.

I live here, I said to myself, this is where I live.

'Well,' she said, 'I go this way. Are you going to walk me home or what?'

She was heading away from Clonduff. There was nothing in that direction. Just country. I didn't expect her to live anywhere except in Clonduff. The disco was for teenagers off the estate. Everybody was off the estate. The only difference was whether you were from the purchased houses or the corporation houses.

'What's up there?'

'My house.'

I was following her. The roads were all new around Clonduff but we were heading into the old roads. The lights stopped being orange. Then we were in darkness, walking where I didn't know.

She was holding my hand.

'Smell,' she said.

I smelled the air but there was nothing special.

'Wait a while and you'll get it,' she said, then: 'Do you read books?'

'I love reading,' I said.

I squeezed her hand. That felt more real than kissing.

'Me too,' she said. 'I love Stephen King and James Herbert.'

I asked her if she'd ever read Jacqueline Susann, but she hadn't.

'I've never read James Herbert,' I said.

'We should swop,' she said. 'I'll give you James Herbert. You give me Jacqueline Susann.'

She stopped. 'Smell now,' she said. 'Have a good whiff.'

She took a big smell of the air, so I did too. This time I got it. A horrible stink.

I said *ugh* and she laughed.

'It's the pig shed. It means we're half way there.'

She found the smell of the pig shed funnier than I did.

'Sometimes when it's windy the smell comes right up to our house. It comes in the windows at night. I tell my sister that Mickey and Pat are coming to get us and she gets scared.'

'Who's Mickey and Pat?'

'They're the pig farmers. They're dead.'

I laughed a bit but I was thinking about how I wanted my life to be more like Jacqueline Susann and less like Mickey and Pat and the pig farm.

I'd only just discovered Jacqueline Susann and I didn't expect to meet anybody else who'd read her books (beside my mother). But Angela acted like reading Jacqueline Susann was the most normal thing in the world, and now she was going to borrow my *Valley of the Dolls*. It was amazing.

'My mother works in the shop in Greenlawn,' I told her. 'Near the Library.'

'I wish my mother worked,' she said. 'She's always around the house, cleaning and moaning. She only reads magazines. My dad reads books but not ones I'd read.'

We walked on for a while, holding hands. It was really cold now and all the heat seemed to be in our hands where they touched. I didn't know what I felt about all this. I hadn't had a girlfriend before for various reasons. A car turned on the road ahead. Its lights lit up bushes, hedges and trees. It was like a space ship. She let my hand go.

'It's probably my dad.' Her voice was worried. 'I was

supposed to telephone him.'

All I could see was silvery white from the headlights and then the car slowed down and stopped right beside us, all shiny and black. The door opened and a man's voice came out.

'It's a bit late to be walking home, isn't it?'

'Sorry,' said Angela, 'I didn't mean...'

Her voice just sort of stopped and she pushed me in the back seat and got in the front herself. The car was big. There was a smell of polish.

'Will you give John a lift home?' she said. He turned around to me and his voice was really deep.

'Where do you live, son?'

'He only lives in Clonduff,' said Angela.

'I didn't ask you,' he said. 'Well?'

I felt funny. He had a big moustache.

'Clonduff.'

'Angela knows she's supposed to call us from the phone box and we'd pick her up. Isn't that right, Angela?' He kept looking at me even though he was talking to Angela.

'The phone box wasn't working.'

'The phone box wasn't working? Sure that's terrible,' he said, sounding like he didn't believe her.

Angela said nothing. She was different now. Like she was afraid to be who she really was with her father around and she had to pretend to be somebody she actually wasn't.

He turned around then and started driving the car.

We were all quiet for a while. You could see the cats' eyes in the road.

I said to drop me off at the top of the estate but they went on going right to my house with me giving the directions. The streets were empty. It felt to me like something had changed and it was to do with Angela's dad and getting a lift home off him. Part of me actually wanted to stay in the car forever with the two of them driving around but another part of me was dying to get out. It felt like we were all sad for a while, then we were there.

Angela had to get out first to let me out.

'Which is your house?'

I pointed at my door.

'I'll call for you on Sunday,' she whispered.

I whispered back ok.

The car moved off, leaving me on the road. It was starting to rain. I could see it falling in the pools of orange. I let myself in. My mother was dozing beside the last bit of the fire. The telly was on with the sound down.

She sort of stretched herself awake and asked me where I'd been so late. I said the disco.

She looked as if she was going to say something to annoy me but she didn't, so I just said goodnight and went upstairs.

◆

I woke up next morning to the sound of my mother cutting the grass in the back. Cutting the grass meant she was in a good mood. And when she was in a good mood I was in a good mood. Things could get complicated with my mother. She had actually bribed me into going to the disco at Clonduff House in the first place by saying she'd get me a stereo for Christmas but I definitely knew she wouldn't want me to tell her what happened after the disco, I mean going off with Angela and everything.

She'd like that I met a girl but not the rest.

The thing was that sometimes she felt like my friend and sometimes my enemy and she was really moody and sometimes we didn't talk.

The lawn mower stopped and then I heard her coming up the stairs.

'Wake up! I need you to go to the shops. It's a lovely morning.'

I said ok and off she went. Then I could hear her in her bedroom muttering to herself, but not in an annoyed way.

She was different to other mothers because of my father. I knew all about sex but my mother's bedroom was a mystery. I sometimes dreamed about my father coming in and him talking to me and my mother and just being around like as if he wasn't dead and in the grave.

Thinking of my father made me think of Angela's father. Him turning up in the car was a bit like a dream, like he wasn't a real person at all, like he'd come out of nowhere in his big car. Maybe someday a car would stop and my own father would open the door and I'd get in. Just on a road somewhere. I knew this could never really happen. He was a rotten skeleton in his coffin. I wanted him to be alive in heaven but I didn't really believe all that. Sometimes God felt like a good idea but usually he didn't.

And, in any way, my father didn't have a car. He had a bike and a car killed him.

I stuck my foot out from under the covers. It was cold. I was trying not to masturbate all the time because my penis was sore. My mother called my penis my man. One day she suddenly told me everything about sex except what happens if you're bent. She said your man is actually called your penis. I knew all of it anyway and I didn't want to talk right then because *Star Trek* was on. The one with the screaming skulls.

Anyway, my penis was sore because I put ointment called Deep Heat on it to see what it felt like. That was one of the reasons why I didn't want Angela to touch me.

I went to the toilet and brushed my teeth. I could hear my mother downstairs singing a song. I wanted to put the Kate Bush album on as soon as I went downstairs. She was my favourite now. Then Gloria Gaynor. I meant to ask Angela about music. My mother liked Gloria Gaynor too. The Gloria Gaynor was actually hers although I'd made a tape of it for my bedroom.

I got dressed, trying not to look in the mirror, and then I went downstairs. My mother turned on the vacuum cleaner as soon as I got in the kitchen so it was too noisy to talk and I definitely couldn't put the Kate Bush on because there was no point.

I was wondering when she was going to go to work so I'd get some peace when she turned off the hoover and actually said 'I'm going to work.' She told me there was frozen chips and fish fingers and beans for me to make for my dinner, she'd be home at six, and there was money and a list of messages on the table, not to forget, and to be careful with the chip pan.

I said goodbye. Then I turned up the record player as high as it would go, pressed play, and lay on the floor and did my sit-ups. When I was finished I had a banana and an apple even though I didn't like fruit. Then I took out four fish fingers and two handfuls of chips and put them in a plastic bag from the drawer of bags. I opened a tin of beans and emptied half of it into the bag and then put the rest of the beans into a bowl and put it in the fridge. Then I tied the bag and put it inside another bag and then I got my jacket and the money for the messages and I went out to the shops.

I flung the food into the bin down at the phone box on the edge of the park. The door was missing off the phone box and Pauline, the one with the bubblegum on her face, was actually in there talking on the phone but she didn't notice me and I didn't want her to.

I actually hated the Clonduff shops. They were full of people I didn't like and the lady behind the counter always had a look of pity when she served me. Everybody else got a smile. Sometimes I walked into the village to the Greenlawn shops (where the people didn't mind me so much) but it took ages and the buses never came. I hadn't done anything to deserve the hate in the Clonduff shops. It was just there. I didn't fit in and people could see it. Maybe I didn't want to fit in, but it made my life hard so I would have if I could.

The weird thing was that they knew whose son I was in the Clonduff shops (i.e. my mother's) and they got on with her but that didn't make any difference. My mother didn't notice any of this. She didn't know how glad I was that the clocks had changed a few weeks ago because it meant more darkness and therefore I could be invisible.

I could never tell her this stuff.

'Tell your mam there'll be power cuts this week,' the lady said when she gave me the change. 'And make sure there's candles and a torch in the house.'

'Alright,' I said, then off I went.

There was nobody around to throw stones. The whole place was empty. Sometimes I imagined a comet that made everybody except me die. This time I imagined Angela would be alive too and we'd be in love and raise the new human race. Maybe I was in love with Angela in reality and we'd eventually get married. I found it hard to imagine people actually had sexual intercourse with each other and babies being born and everything. It was like a weird joke.

Everybody wandering around in their normal trousers and skirts and underneath them their sexual organs were waiting.

There was a funeral at the church. The flowers spelt out NAN. It started to rain a bit. I didn't have a nan so I said a prayer to my father. Please let me lose weight. Please let me not be bent.

The day of my father's funeral it rained and my mother stepped in a puddle when she got out of the car. She wasn't crying or anything but she hurt my arm where she held on. There was a bruise that night. I'd never seen my mother and father kiss or hug so that was why my eyes watered a bit, because I would never be able to make that happen. I wanted to be able to make them be like people in films and books but that just wasn't the way it was. Nothing in my life was like that.

The only other funeral I'd ever been at was for the father of a boy at school. The whole class went and we sat in the back and the boy was at the front. I remember seeing him when I went to communion and thinking how saintly he looked.

But I don't think I looked saintly at my father's funeral. Driving around in that big black car, I felt as if something important had finally happened to me.

I liked being in cars and I knew that if my father had been in a car he wouldn't be dead. It made me not like bicycles that much anymore even though I had one.

Thinking all this made the walk home quicker but as soon as I got in I realised I was starving hungry so I got the Slender from my wardrobe and made a drink. It was about one o'clock. I put on the Gloria Gaynor and did my sit-ups. Then I just lay on the ground breathing hard.

The coalman came so I got up and answered the door. He was covered in coal and had a big sack of it. He was always friendly. He came through the house and put the coal in the shed. The leg of his trousers was ripped and you could see the skin where it wasn't covered in coal. I gave him the money and off he went.

After that I ran really hot water in the bath and got in. It made my skin go red under the water. I put lots of bubble bath in to make the water blue then I lay back and thought about how hot the coalman's bath would be when he got home and how the water would be all dirty from the coal when he got out.

Then I read until it was an hour before my mother came home and then I got to work. First I lit the fire and when it was definitely lit I peeled the potatoes and put them on the gas. She liked to have a rasher and egg and mashed potato when she came home from work on a Saturday. I made her a cup of tea when she came in. I liked looking after her on Saturdays. We always watched telly together and the film later.

She brought me my *Films Illustrated*. She was tired. She was nearly always tired nowadays but she ate all her dinner. She said I'd make somebody a lovely wife someday.

◆

'I hope that's nobody.' It was the next day. My mother had ice cream around her mouth.

I went to the door and there was Angela. She had a bike with her. She looked different in her Sunday clothes and her hair in a ponytail.

My mother was wiping the ice cream off her lips. She stood up. Sometimes she didn't act like the grown-up at all. She had her navy polka dot dress on. Sometimes, if I looked at this dress I could imagine I was looking into space or infinity. Sometimes if I looked at things for ages I could see the atoms and molecules vibrating and moving around. It reminded me that everything was just mush in the end. I knew this from science but I knew it anyway before the teacher told me.

'Hello,' said my mother. It was a funny five seconds that came next but nothing much happened. Angela and my mother just looked at each other, I suppose.

Then I said this is Angela and I grabbed her and pushed her toward the stairs.

'We're going up to my room.'

'Ok,' said Angela. 'Keep your knickers on.'

'You'll need to turn on the fire. It's cold up there and I don't want that girl freezing to death in my house. I don't mind about you.'

I was already wheeling the superser into my bedroom.

'I like your mother better than mine,' said Angela. 'Mine's crap.'

This was the second time that she'd said her mother was crap. I asked her if she liked her father.

'My sister and my mam hate him, but I don't,' she said. She asked me about my father so I told her he was dead, and she said she was sorry. I said how he got run over on the bike. I could see him on the ground when I was telling her. His bike scrunched up beside him. Dead as a doornail. Dad as a doornail. I wasn't sure why but I liked saying that. It made my father into a piece of old wood, like a fallen tree with one nail hammered into it and a trickle of blood coming out of it and trickling down onto the road where it made a little pool.

'It's ok,' I was saying. 'Me and my mother are ok. We look after each other.'

Then I put the Gloria Gaynor on.

Angela had a packet of mints and two cigarettes.

She asked if I had any David Bowie and I said I didn't and she looked a bit disappointed. We smoked out the window.

It was beginning to get dark and you could see into all the back gardens along the block.

'The gardens look sad,' she said. 'There should be people in them. It makes me depressed.'

I dragged on my cigarette.

'How can looking at gardens make you depressed?' I said.

'I had a row at home,' she said. 'My dad prefers my sister to me and, even though she hates him, he lets her away with everything. My mother was crying and everything.'

'I'd like a sister,' I said. 'But I'm glad I don't have a brother.' This was true. I didn't like other boys. They were different to me, like a different species on an alien planet I'd been dropped on and abandoned.

The lights in the back lane came on. Everything looked lonely. We just smoked for a while, listening to the music.

Angela was reading the lyrics.

'I want to be a writer,' she said.

'Me too,' I said.

'Maybe we should write a book together. Or poems or something,' she said.

She looked through my books for a while and we just talked and laughed about stuff, nothing in particular, just stuff that we were interested in and things we had in common.

My mother called up the stairs when it was tea time and asked if Angela wanted to stay but Angela said no, that she had to get home.

We went downstairs to say goodbye.

'Well, it was lovely to meet you, Angela. You take care cycling home.' I could tell my mother was glad that I had somebody (i.e. a girl) in the house.

It was cold out and there was a gang of boys hanging around at the end of the road.

'That's Paul. From the other night,' said Angela.

I looked but I couldn't really tell which one she meant although I knew she was talking about the one who raped her, and I didn't want him to see me staring and know where I live so I just pretended I saw him.

'He takes magic mushrooms. That's why he killed the horse.'

I wasn't completely sure what magic mushrooms were so I just moved my head up and down.

And then she was on her bike going up the road in the dark. She cycled right through the gang of boys. One of them shouted something at her and she turned and gave him the fingers, and then she was gone.

When I went back inside, my mother asked me where Angela lived. I just said on the back roads. Neither of us said anything then and I went upstairs with my mug of tea and a sandwich. I didn't have any biscuits or cake.

◆

I did ok at school. There was a time when I did really well. That was gone but I managed to stay in the A class. I sat beside a boy who was always sick. I liked him because he wasn't good at sport either but we didn't kick around together or anything outside school. He had brittle bones. His name was Brendan Blake. He had an older brother who liked David Bowie.

I looked out the window a lot. The sky was usually grey or silver. Break time I'd talk to Brendan about telly. Sometimes I was called a fairy or a bender but there were other boys who got it worse. I avoided them. Liam Kelly called me fatboy. Lunchtime, I went to the amusements in town to play video games or went to bookshops. My mother made me sandwiches. I only ate half of them except on gym days.

Monday came and went. The weather was damp and grey and when it got dark it rained and the wind blew like hell. Mornings, I woke up with my breath coming out like smoke. The whole week was the same. I got out of bed in the morning thinking about getting back into bed that night.

The superser was on nearly all the time.

Halfway through the week we had a power cut and my mother and me sat up playing cards. She drank her brandy and I drank my lemonade. We had cheese and onion sandwiches. I had a sip of brandy when she wasn't looking but she knew anyway. Her face went from old to young and then to really old in the candle light. She had crow's feet. I didn't do my homework and I got into trouble at school but I didn't care. Kate Bush was in the charts. I ate a half a pound of peanuts all to myself and then I made myself sick.

I prayed to my father to be thin and normal and not to

be hopeless at everything.

One of the nights, my mother and I had a row because I didn't want to go up to the village to pay the credit union. I put the Gloria Gaynor on really loud. Then we had a dance and a laugh and off I went to the credit union. It was a miserable night so there was nobody around on the way to the village. It was a bit scary going through the park and there were lights on in Clonduff House and vampire bats flitting around in the dark but they didn't actually bother me.

Then Saturday morning came and the sky was blue, really blue. The kind of blue my mother called virgin blue. The Virgin Mary statue in my mother's bedroom had a blue and white cloak on but this blue in the sky was a different blue so I wasn't actually sure what virgin blue was.

I told my mother I was going to the library and she asked where my library books were.

Under my breath I said o fuck off but out loud I said I only needed to look something up for school so I wasn't bringing any books. She looked at me like she didn't believe me and off I went.

Boys were playing football on the road in the direction I wanted to go so I had to turn back on myself and go through the playground that never had anybody playing in it and then down the side of the estate. You could see the back of my house from there, the backs of all the houses. You could actually see my bedroom window.

Clonduff Estate was its own little world. It all seemed normal and at the same time when I looked at all the other bedroom windows the exact same as mine and thought about the fact that there was a person whose day ended when they got into their bedroom at night and closed the curtains and put on their pyjamas and went asleep and had dreams, when I thought like that it made me feel the way I tried to feel but didn't when I went to mass. It made me feel like there was something going on that you couldn't see. It wasn't necessarily something bad either but it was a sad feeling in a way, because you could never really know the thing that was going on or if it was real or if you made it up because you were mad. I thought about Angela and how the empty gardens made her depressed. My feeling wasn't like being depressed. It was more like a loneliness for the whole world and everybody in it, a loneliness that the whole world felt but nobody could do anything about.

The wind had picked up and huge, ice-cream clouds were twirling around in the sky. A boy at school called his sperm his cream. I walked along the grass bit. There was a million sperm in every teaspoon. There was nobody around so I sang Gloria Gaynor.

I wasn't sure how I was going to find Angela's house

but I knew there wasn't many houses on the old roads. I had driven back here before when my Uncle Brian brought me and my mother for a drive when we first moved. I knew the pig shed was half way there. But that was all I knew.

The creamy clouds were gone and now it was just grey like the inside of my lunch box for school or the box we kept the biscuits in.

I was glad I had songs but I was running out of them by the time I got a whiff of the pig shed. It was just an old building by the side of the road with a tin roof. It stank and a dog barked. I could hear an engine going somewhere, maybe a tractor or something, but I couldn't see anything moving.

The gate was rusty and brown bits of it rubbed off on my hands when I touched it, a kind of sparkly brown. The shed was open at one end with just a wooden fence to stop you getting in but you couldn't actually see inside and I couldn't hear any oinks. The pigs were probably gone now that the farmers were dead.

Further up the field there was an ancient old farmhouse and a falling apart caravan, a dirty pink colour, with smoke coming out of its chimney. The engine sound was coming from there somewhere but there was nothing else to see really and the smell was horrible so I went on.

I started singing Kate Bush. They weren't easy songs. My mother didn't like her. It was the first time we didn't like the same music and it annoyed me.

I kept going until I saw a house ahead so I stopped singing and slowed down a bit. Maybe this was it but it didn't seem the right distance and sure enough when I got near I could see an old man standing in the garden in front of the house. This house was too small and this man was too old and there was no car parked. I remembered the car was big and that didn't fit with this house either. Nothing was right so I went on. The old man moved his head up and down at me as I walked by so I did the same back.

The road turned ahead. A bike came round the bend. A girl was on it. It wasn't Angela. It was a racing bike and she swooshed past without even looking at me. You could feel the speed of the bike and hear the wheels go around but at the same time everything seemed like it was in slow motion too.

Then the girl on the bike was gone and I turned the next bend and I saw three houses close together. One of these must be Angela's, I thought. There was a squashed dog or fox on the ground with flies buzzing around it.

This was definitely a good sign and everything seemed a bit different here anyway and the air was thicker and darker like it was going to rain. I could see a lady doing something in a shed down the side of the first house and a dog on a chain in the garden was growling and slobbering so I moved on because Angela had told me her dog was really friendly and hardly ever growled or needed to be on the lead.

The next house was bigger and newer. It was a bungalow. It had long glass windows and you could see inside where it was all brown wood and cluttered with stuff and kind of untidy right to the back windows. The rooms were big and I could see a long brown sofa and a big telly. It made me think of houses on American TV shows. It looked nothing like the type of house that I lived in except it had a door and windows and a roof and a chimney.

I decided it had to be this one so I opened the gate and went up the path. There was two little bushes in pots on either side of the door. I could hear a radio somewhere but it was just men talking about sport or politics or something. Suddenly I didn't want to knock but I did anyway.

Approximately twenty five seconds passed before a woman came to the door. She looked like a man with long hair. She was wearing jeans and men's boots and a man's t-shirt. She looked like she didn't do much laughing and joking.

'Come in, come in,' she said, as if she was expecting me, as if she knew I was coming,

'Angela's upstairs. She's too lazy to answer the door.'

I must have looked funny because she smiled suddenly and then her face kind of softened and I could see that she was Angela's mother. They both had extra long necks.

She gave me a sign to go up the stairs. I didn't realise there was an upstairs when I looked at the house on the outside but, sure enough, there was, so up I went.

'I'm back here, John.' It was Angela's voice alright.

The top of the stairs was a narrow landing. There was loads of shoes along the wall, mainly runners and boots, no high heels. There was an open door at the end.

'I'm in here.'

I went in. The ceiling was an upside down V.

Angela was sitting on the floor beside a dog lying on a blanket. It was a big room and there was loads of books on shelves. There was a poster of a popstar I didn't know and a map of the world. The room smelled of dog and the windows were in the roof. One of these was open so that it looked like there was a gap where rain could come in. There was a big telescope so you could look at the stars but it would have to be night time.

'This is Timmy,' she said. 'He's just had an operation. He only came back yesterday from the vet.'

The dog looked up at me from his raggedy blanket.

I said hello and he wagged his tail. He was a mixture

of colours.

'He likes you,' said Angela. 'He's bisexual. You can pet him but only his head. He's sore. He had a tumour in his stomach.'

She got up and put a record on. It was Kate Bush. I couldn't remember if we'd talked about it so I told her I loved Kate Bush. She did too. She said music was the language of the heart and that Kate Bush was a genius. We listened to the Kate Bush record, both of us petting the dog and sitting on the floor. Angela had her eyes closed. Her skin was perfect and she had no freckles or pimples.

When the song was over she opened her eyes again.

'I'm glad you found the house,' she said. 'I dreamed you were here last night petting Timmy just like what's actually happening now. I get a lot of dreams that come true.'

I told her about my dreams that my father came home like it was a normal day and he was alive and everything was back to normal.

She said nothing but I was used to people saying nothing when I talked about my father so I just lay down beside the dog and looked at the sky through the window. It was nice knowing the dog was right beside me. I was thinking that I was a bit disappointed that Angela was like everybody else (i.e. not wanting me to talk about my dead father) when suddenly she actually asked me what my dead father's name was.

'Michael,' I said.

'My dad's called Mick,' she said.

I looked up. 'Sometimes my mother called my father Mick,' I said, 'but usually it's just Michael. It's written on his gravestone.'

'Do you visit his grave much?'

'Every few weeks.'

The truth was I didn't really like going to the grave. I didn't like seeing my mother move her lips when she was praying and no words coming out. It looked like she was taken over by something, like in a horror film. It gave me the creeps. I imagined that if she said the words she was saying under her breath out loud they would be words I didn't understand or even like the sound of.

So it was nothing to do with my father being dead and actually rotting in the ground underneath us that made me not want to go to his grave. That was just part of things, like growing hair on your testicles or vagina. Weird, but not from a horror film.

'Was that your mother who answered the door?' I asked this question even though I already knew the answer.

'Yeah.'

I said nothing although I felt like Angela expected me to. It started raining outside and the rain actually came through the window so she got up and got a special stick with a hook on the end and closed it. The dog watched her. She was really slim.

'She used to be a receptionist in a hotel but now she's always sick.'

'Who?'

'My mother, stupid.'

I said oh and then I asked why she (i.e. Angela's mother) was always sick.

'Her nerves,' said Angela. 'My father and her fight all the time. She has to take tranquilisers.'

She lay down with the back of her head on my shins.

'Why did you not like us kissing the other night?'

'I did like it,' I said. My voice went really high.

Neither of us said anything for approximately thirty seconds.

'Are you bisexual?'

She asked the question as if the answer to it was the easiest answer in the world.

'Maybe,' I said.

I was acting as if it was ordinary to be talking like this.

'Me and my sister are definitely bisexual,' said Angela.

We said nothing for approximately fifteen seconds. My face was hot and I felt a bit scared. But more of what was inside me waiting to be said than scared of Angela for asking about it. This feeling was in my stomach.

Then Angela said, 'It's ok to not want to kiss girls.'

I said nothing because I didn't know what to say and then we were quiet for approximately another thirty seconds and I watched the rain fall on the sideways window and roll down it. I liked the feeling of this. It made me forget about the feeling in my stomach.

Then I said that if I lived there I would have windscreen wipers put on the windows. We laughed a bit, and then we stopped laughing.

Angela got up and put on a different record. This music was really loud and I wasn't sure I liked it.

She handed me the album cover. It opened out into a big photo of a half man/half dog in a futuristic freak show. It was called *Diamond Dogs*.

'He's a genius,' she said. 'David Bowie.'

She got up and did an impression of somebody playing a guitar. Timmy started whining. I kissed him on the head, inhaling his doggy smell, glad he wasn't half David Bowie. He licked my hand. It was still sparkly brown from the rusty gate at the pig farm. Now there was sparkles on his tongue.

Angela kept doing her guitar dance and pretending to sing into a microphone.

Timmy watched her. All one side of him was shaved and you could see stitches like two bits of meat sewn together.

All of a sudden I wanted to go home.

She said to stay. She said we could have beans on toast but for some reason the thought of that made me want to go even more. I got my coat.

'Carrie is on at the Olympia.' We were going down the stairs. 'They let you in there even if it's over eighteens. Do you want to go?'

I said yes and she said she'd call for me tomorrow after twelve o'clock mass and then off I went.

I was glad to be gone. It was raining a bit but it wasn't very cold and I didn't mind. I liked it. It calmed me down. The squashed dog or fox was still there. You could see bits of its insides. Flies were on it. A wasp was zigzagging. It made me think of this ghost story from when I was young about these children who are minding this old house for a lady and she tells them they can do anything and eat anything and drink anything except they can't go into this particular room. Anyway, they go into the room and the lady is in the nude and she's dancing with the devil and there's livers and kidneys and hearts and blood all over the gaff and the devil captures their souls and drags them into hell for ever. And if you go into that house now you can see their shadows moving on the floors and walls and you can hear them roaring and crying all night.

I got to the pig farm really fast. There was a bike locked to the gate.

I imagined it was Angela's sister and she was having an adventure.

I'd seen a film about girls getting into trouble when they were on holiday somewhere on their bikes and they were raped and strangled in an old caravan.

I took a big whiff of the pig shed. The smell wasn't that bad once you got used to it.

◆

The next morning I got up early and off we went to mass. It was a horrible day, damp and grey, and I didn't want to be anywhere near a church but, more than that, I didn't want an argument. I knew when to be careful with my mother.

I felt a bit sorry for her. I'd heard her in the middle of the night talking to herself in the bedroom. I couldn't hear what she was saying but it sounded sad. I called in to see if she was alright but she just said yes she was and that I was to go back to sleep. I did and then I had the usual dream about my father being back in the house and everything being normal.

Things got better after mass when we were getting the dinner ready. The radio was on and the songs put her in a good mood. She knew loads of old songs and it was a good sign to hear her sing along. It always made me think of the photograph in the box of photographs in the wardrobe where she looked like a film star or something.

Here was my mother before she got married and had me, when she went to the pictures all the time and had friends. It was like a magical time.

Of course loads of the photos in the wardrobe had my father in them and I didn't want to look at them. But my mother was alive and well and I let myself look at her photos and anyway she had a life even before my father got married to her.

All of this was ordinary enough until I really thought about it, then it could make the world seem very weird.

For example, I hated being alive on school mornings and I actually hated my mother for making me get out of bed and always going on about how important school was. I hated her even more because she'd never admit how horrible and miserable it was to have to get up on a rainy morning even though she usually looked more miserable than anybody else. But when I looked at some of the photographs in that box I could tell there was a part of my mother that wanted to stay in bed, that wanted to be a film star or a millionaire, that wanted everything to be like being on holidays. And I saw it too when she watched films on telly or even sometimes when she was singing songs from musicals or just sitting at her dressing table putting Nivea on her face or Atrixo on her hands.

But she was afraid to admit it.

This was a bit like a lie and living a lie was supposed to be a sin.

And then she went to mass and I don't think she thought of herself as a liar at all.

In a way, I could see inside my mother and what I saw was a film star or a millionaire wanting to get out.

But Sunday was always a little bit like a holiday anyway and by the time we sat down to have our dinner everything seemed ok with her. And, as I said previously, when everything was ok with her, everything was ok with me. We didn't actually talk much. The radio was on with her favourite DJ doing his show.

Angela came around when we were washing up. My mother asked her things like how old she was and where she went to school and where she lived. I knew Angela liked my mother, but watching them talk I wasn't sure that my mother liked her back. I could see that she was glad Angela was here and she was my friend and everything but there was something in her eyes that made me wonder if she actually wished Angela would just leave us alone to have our normal Sunday.

It was lashing rain when me and Angela left for the pictures. We ran down to the bus stop and got there just on time. There was only one an hour on Sundays. Angela's hair was plastered to her head when we got on the bus. I liked it like that.

I had twenty Kingsize and I could tell she was impressed when I took them out.

'You know you have the same eyes as your mother,' she said, lighting my cigarette.

I'd heard people talk about the colour of peoples' eyes before but I never actually noticed anything like that about anybody before this. I looked right into Angela's eyes and I could see they were greeny brown and had little blue flecks in them. She crossed them for me and we broke our hearts.

I told her she had nice eyes.

'Don't push your luck,' she said.

The rain pelted on the bus windows all the way to the cinema and I was happy. The streets were wet and shiny and the cinema was all lit up when we got there. We bought sweets and drinks and the tickets and went in. It was actually two over 18s films and I was nervous that we wouldn't get in but we did. The woman said nothing at all. The place smelled of popcorn and it was a bit old and falling down. The inside was dark red.

The first film was *Carrie* about the telekinetic girl who

wreaks havoc on her neighbourhood. She has her period in the showers and the other girls laugh at her. Angela said *ugh* when she saw the blood but I didn't. It was from the book that we both loved so we were really interested in it. In the end there was a big shock that made us jump out of our skin but I won't ruin it by saying what it is.

We smoked and chatted through the intermission. I was really happy and Angela was too.

The second film was *Alien* with the thing bursting out of the man's stomach and the woman blowing up the ship and escaping in the little ship with the alien still on board and her in her underwear. At the end though the alien looked all rubbery and shaped like the devil and that was disappointing. People in America were getting sick and running out of the cinema roaring and crying because they were so scared but me and Angela didn't think it was that great.

The woman in *Alien* reminded me of Angela's mother but when I told Angela this she looked at me like I was mad. Smoke came out of her mouth. She liked that I knew about the films before we saw them. (This was because I'd read my *Films Illustrated*.) There was little lights with fancy lampshades in the wall everywhere but the bulbs weren't strong and some of them weren't even working so everything was dark. A man was looking at us when we came out at the end, thinking they're very young to be watching films like this. We laughed in his face and ran out into the rain with our cigarettes.

Then we got the bus back in the rain, talking about films and books. I didn't care about who was on the bus or whether they were looking at us. Sometimes when the buses were quiet and it was dark and I was by myself I was quite worried, but not this night.

When we got back to Clonduff it was miserable and windy. We ran to my house. There was always stones and bits of bricks and broken glass on the roads and it was hard to tell where they actually came from. Sometimes stones that boys threw at you whizzed past your ear when you were walking around, but not usually glass.

My mother was home and gave out to us for getting wet and not having an umbrella. The fire was lit and she gave us two chicken sandwiches and cake on a plate and two mugs of tea. She was watching the telly so we went upstairs to eat the food and listen to tapes. I ate the sandwich but Angela had all the cake.

Later on, she phoned her house and her father came to pick her up. He didn't come in and I didn't see him this time. Angela said thanks to my mother and goodbye to me then ran out the door and jumped into the car. Part of me wanted to be going with her but the other part was glad to be in my house.

◆

Monday to Friday was school for me, work for my mother. The house was freezing and it was miserable and raining when we were waiting for the bus. Clonduff was grey grey grey in the mornings and even though there was plenty of fields everywhere most of them had houses being built on them. There was bricks and tiles everywhere. Sometimes I felt like I was in the middle of somewhere like Siberia or something.

In religion, the teacher told us that not believing in God was the same as believing that the bricks that made up the school ran down the road and made themselves into a school of their own free will. Brendan Blake said religion was the opium of the masses. Dermot Doyle wanted to be a priest. Everyone called him a spa.

I started to say ClonduffSiberia in my head when I was thinking about the estate. Everybody at school came from nearby but I had to come in everyday from ClonduffSiberia. On Tuesday when I got home to ClonduffSiberia there was a man in the house. I thought maybe he was somebody who used to work with my father. Sometimes we had visitors like that. He had a mug of tea and a biscuit and off he went. But when he was gone my mother told me he was from the tenants association and she was going to be on the committee.

She said his name was Mr Daly.

My mother was in a funny mood nearly all week.

After my father died we were the best of friends for about a year and we spent all our time together. It was a bit like we were the children and my father was the father and we had to prove to the outside world that we were alright now that he was dead. We listened to records and watched telly and read books, but then something changed and my mother went all quiet and started crying a lot at night. She said the records were old and scratched and they actually were but that hadn't been a problem before.

It was around this time that she applied for the house in Clonduff. It took about a year for it to come through and that year we didn't really get on like we did the first year he died. We spent evenings not talking, just reading or she'd be staring at the wall. Things got better when we moved and that was probably because my father actually never lived in the new house but there were times when it all looked bad again.

But even though my mother was in a funny mood nearly all week, I could tell that she was sort of pleased when I got a phone call from Angela. It was the first phone call I ever got in the house in Clonduff. I was reading my book by the fire and my mother was doing the cleaning when the phone went and it was Angela. I'd been meaning to telephone her because we were supposed to go out to the disco on the Friday but anyway she phoned me instead so that was that.

She sounded in trouble and she told me she wasn't allowed to go to the disco. When I asked her why she said her sister had run away, that the gardai were looking for her, and she hadn't come home since Saturday.

I thought of the girl that whizzed past on the bike when I was going up to Angela's house. That was Saturday. I could feel the second when she went past me really fast on her racing bike and me wondering if she was Angela's sister. But I wasn't sure so I said nothing.

Angela told me her sister had run away before and the gardai had found her on a bus going down the country to her cousins.

'She does it for attention.'

I was in the hall, sitting on the floor looking at a spider crawling along the carpet. I took off my slipper and swatted it until it was all rolled up and dead.

I asked her what her sister's name was.

'Marion.'

The spider came back from the dead and ran off.

'I think Marion will come back, Angela,' I said, 'and I think you'll be glad to see her.'

'What makes you think that?'

'I don't know. I just feel it.'

And I did just feel it, and just then it was the truth. But it was the truth based on the fact that the spider came back to life.

Angela said she'd telephone me again because she thought her mam and dad would change their minds about her going out on Friday.

I said I didn't mind not going out and we could go around to one of our houses and just listen to music and talk.

When I got off the phone my mother asked me who it was.

She didn't say anything when I told her it was Angela, just got on with the ironing, but she started humming a song, ironing away, and then all of a sudden she said: 'Why don't you get that old bike out of the shed and have a go on it?'

I hadn't been on the bike much since my father got killed.

'I don't really want to,' I said.

'Ah, you're useless,' she said.

This meant I better give it a go so when I finished my chapter I got the shed key out of the drawer by the sink.

The shed had a big box of coal, the toolbox that my mother still called 'your father's tool box' (I sometimes called it 'my father's tool box' when I was thinking about it in my head but I never said this out loud, and I wanted to ask my mother why she didn't call it 'my husband's tool box' but I never did), loads of half-empty tins of paint, the lawn mower, the shovel, the pick axe, the old budgie's cage (quite rusty), millions of spiders and loads of spider webs and a musty smell I liked, and my old bike in the middle of it all.

It wasn't a racer but it had three gears.

I hadn't meant to stop cycling after my father died but my mother got really worried every time I went anywhere on the bike and it got on my nerves and we had a big fight about it and that was that.

I pulled it out backwards by the saddle, knocking a load of tins of paint over but they didn't spill. I waited for a second to see if my mother was behind me waiting to pass some remark or give out or something but she wasn't there. I was ready to explode if she started so I was glad she didn't. I wondered if she was watching me from behind the curtains. Sometimes it was like I could do nothing without her poking her nose in.

Once the bike was actually out of the shed I began to feel better and my mind made me think back to the day I went to the bike shop with my father. It was my birthday and he knew the bike shop man and he got a bargain. My father knew everybody. He knew the pet shop man so he got a bargain on the budgie except it turned out to have a bad foot and anyway the thing escaped out the window. We weren't upset or anything. I think my mother was actually glad because she didn't like the budgie that much and I felt like it was better off to be flying around rather than stuck in a cage. But my mother told me that other birds would peck it to death because it was different. It was called Bluey. Sometimes I worried about Bluey and if he was still alive, all pecked and sore and freezing cold on an old branch somewhere. I thought I saw him once in a tree down by the shops but it turned out to be a bit of plastic. Animals crossed continents to follow their owners when they moved. But not Bluey. And he wasn't one of those budgies that talked. Unless he said things to himself in the little mirror when we weren't around.

'The bike'll be good for you, you might lose some of that weight.' It was my mother. Sticking her nose in. The annoying thing was that that she was right, and underneath all my thoughts about Bluey, I was actually thinking about how fat I was and how if I started cycling again and went on a calorie controlled diet then I would be slim.

I looked at her and said I know but not in a cheeky way.

I could tell that she meant well. Sometimes you could hear in my mother's voice that all she really wanted was a happy ending for everybody and everything but then again sometimes you couldn't hear a trace of a happy ending in anything she said or did.

I opened the back gate and got on the bike.

'Be careful,' she shouted.

'I will,' I shouted back. This was one of the times when we both knew that we loved each other.

It wasn't actually raining but the air was wet with ultra-tiny raindrops. It was cold and dark on the bike but it felt good to be balanced on it and going anywhere I wanted. That was the thing I'd forgotten. You felt you could keep going anywhere you liked when you were on your bike. As if you never had to actually stop. A few people were walking around and maybe they were looking at me thinking I was an eejit but I didn't feel useless on a bike, no sirree. It was different to walking around. You felt like you were in a different dimension.

Anyway, I cycled around the estate and then I went back. I had no back brakes and the front ones were useless and I was freezing. But I'd been on the bike and I knew that was a good thing. It meant I would get on it again. Angela and I could go cycling somewhere. I could cycle to her house.

'Well done,' said my mother when I got back. 'You must be freezing. I'll make us a cup of tea.'

I knew something had changed in my mother and maybe in me and all because I was back on the bike. I sat down by the fire and she brought me a cup of tea and a biscuit and she had one herself.

'Next time, keep the bike under the stairs,' she said. 'Not in the shed anymore.'

I said ok.

'It's nice to see you doing so well, son.'

'What do you mean?' I said.

'It's just good to see you back on the bike.'

The fire was lovely and warm.

I threw the biscuit in when she went to the toilet.

It was one of those biscuits with pink gooey stuff on it like a little cushion.

It bubbled first and unusual yellow and blue flames came out of it, then it all went black and then it disappeared and there was just the big orangey fire burning like normal.

◆

Friday came and Marion was still missing. Angela phoned and said her mother and father had calmed down and she wasn't being kept in like a prisoner anymore. She said her father would give her a lift down to my house and we could listen to music and stuff. We wanted to start writing our novel anyway. Then her father spoke to my mother and my mother spoke back to him in the voice she kept for people who were rich or priests or doctors or teachers. I didn't like this voice. I already knew she was off to the tenants' association that night so it meant me and Angela could go out as soon as she was gone and she'd never know once we were back before she was. Also, she didn't go o my God or anything so I guessed that Angela's father hadn't said anything about the sister going missing.

We'd done some thinking about our novel but all we really knew was that it was about a passage in time that led back to a prehistoric world where aliens were operating on monkeys to make them intelligent so the human race could begin. Two girls go back to free the monkeys and because they're from the future they know the human race is ok but when they free the monkeys from the experiments and return to the present, they find that the human race has never existed because they have changed history and now the world is run by a race of vampires and they have to go on the run but luckily they've been impregnated by the aliens in an experiment and now their children will be the saviours of civilisation, sort of half human and half alien.

I'd seen a programme on telly about these people who were pretending to live in the Iron Age. They went around in the nude and killed animals for food. They hung a pig upside down and slashed its throat open. Blood squirted everywhere. Then there was these experiments that

Angela had seen on telly where they took baby monkeys away from their mothers and put them in cages by themselves with no sounds and where they saw nobody, and nobody ever touched them, and the baby monkeys went mad or died of boredom and from never being touched. Angela said they died of broken hearts.

These two programmes were our inspiration.

The girls were working as receptionists in Hollywood before they embark on their adventure. The actual passage in time was through the third O in the Hollywood sign.

The problem was where to start the story. We decided on just an ordinary day in work for the girls. Filing and typing. Then a walk in the Hollywood hills when suddenly there's an earthquake and they fall through the third O and get catapulted back in time.

Anyway, we talked about this for a while and then we got bored.

Angela got me to rob some brandy from my mother's bottle and top it up with water. I'd never done that before but it felt like the right thing to do once we came up with the idea. I could only take little sips but Angela was able to take bigger mouthfuls and she had to top up the bottle a couple of times. Anyway, in the end, we decided to go out. We didn't want to go to the disco but Angela said she knew somewhere we could go so off we went.

It was freezing cold. The sky was low and greeny grey.

I looked up at the lights and you could see rain falling sideways. We were in ClonduffSiberia, alright. We had fur around our hoods and we had them up so nobody would be able to tell if we were boys or girls. Sometimes I wondered what the difference actually was between me and girls. Girls got pregnant and had periods and breasts and vaginas. Boys had penises and testicles. I knew all that but deep down what were the differences? Girls were supposed to cry more. Boys wanted fights all the time and liked sport.

But I didn't really see evidence of that in me. Sometimes I wished there were girls in my school. Angela went to a different kind of school to me and there was a mixture of boys and girls there.

She actually knew somebody who used to go to her school who had VD.

'His name is Tony Byrne. He went with Marion after she stopped going with Paul.'

'Has he still got it?'

'The doctor's after giving him a prescription to get rid of it.'

I asked her if Marion was on the pill.

'No, but she knew where to get it. I do too if I want it,' she said, 'but I don't need a boyfriend now that we're friends, so I don't need the pill neither.'

One minute she was really grown up and the next she

wasn't. That was Angela. I wondered if half the stuff she was saying was made up. I didn't really mind because we were friends and that was that. We really liked each other and that was all that mattered.

She stopped to light a cigarette.

'Marion always had boyfriends and she'd be fighting and arguing with them and all I hear in my house is my mam and dad shouting at each other.'

The match kept going out in the wind but after three goes it lit.

'The night before Marion ran away there was a massive row. Next morning she got on her bike and never came back.'

She had a big drag on the cigarette.

'Angela,' I said, 'did your sister have a racing bike?'

I wanted to find out if her sister was the girl on the bike.

'Yeah, why?'

'I think I saw her the day I was up in your house.'

I said I couldn't be sure it was her, that it was just a girl.

Angela said nothing. She looked like she was thinking about things and I didn't get the impression she liked me talking about this stuff.

We were walking down the main road at the side of the estate where you could see all the bedrooms. Some of them had lights on and some of them didn't. On the other side of the road they were building new houses on the fields. Nobody had moved in over there and there was nobody around. The streets weren't actually built. It was just muck and stones, and there was no lights or windows in the houses, and there were JCBs parked around and piles of bricks and big huge spools of thick electric wires everywhere. You couldn't see a lot of this because it was dark. I just knew it was all there.

We crossed over the road. I was following her. I asked where we were going but she only said *sshhh*.

The ground was bumpy so we had to be careful where we were walking and there was bricks and tiles everywhere. We were in where the new houses were. Like the ghosts of big whales at the bottom of the sea, they came out of the dark at you when you didn't expect them to be there and then suddenly there was another one floating around in the dark. It was like all the families were dead or they had to run away suddenly because something terrible had happened. It was creepy with the wind blowing and whistling and weird noises around so I was glad I was with Angela. I thought about us holding hands but I knew that something was different and we wouldn't be doing that again. This didn't make me feel sad or anything.

We went right up to the front door of the house at the

end of one of the blocks and Angela pushed it but it didn't move so she kicked it really hard with a karate kick. It opened this time and we went in. We went through to the back of the house and there was a back door with a glass window in it. There was words painted on the walls but I couldn't make them out. I think this was the kitchen part but it was different to my house. Anyway, this door opened up easy enough and we were in the back garden except it was just a field really. There was a shed here but it was more like a big black box. It was like the opposite of the white houses. Angela seemed to know what she was doing. She went up to it and opened the door. She didn't need to kick this one.

'In you go,' she said.

I went into the black box. It was like walking into a space ship in a science fiction film. Then Angela closed the door behind us and the swirling, whirling wind was locked outside.

It was pitch dark for a second then she turned on a big torch.

We were in the workmen's hut.

There was a table with a gas ring and a kettle and mugs and loads of packets of biscuits and stuff to make tea. There was a superser exactly like the one we had at home and loads of yellow hats and a pile of raingear and newspapers. I could actually see a girl with her blouse off. Angela lit the superser. You could feel the heat nearly right away.

'It's good, isn't it?' she said. She put the torch on the table facing upward.

She took something out of her pocket and held it up. It was two tiny bottles of whiskey. Her face was gone funny. For the first time since I met her I thought she didn't look nice.

'Let's have a drink.'

She got two mugs off the table and poured the drink in. I got out the cigarettes. We clunked our mugs together and lit the cigarettes. She sat in the chair and I sat beside her on the ground.

She got a packet of biscuits off the table and opened them. She took a few and then she gave the pack to me.

I asked her whose biscuits they were.

'Tony who lives here,' she said.

'Tony who has VD?'

'Don't tell him I said that or he'll kill me.'

'Is he cured yet?'

'I told you he's got a prescription off the doctor,' she said, and then we both started breaking our hearts and we were still laughing when, all of a sudden, there was a bang on the door of the hut and then it just flew open and somebody walked in. We both stopped laughing straight away and there was a weird feeling in the air and I could see that Angela was a bit worried.

She made her mouth say the word *Tony* at me without actually making any noise, just the shapes of the word on her mouth and lips.

Tony was tall and skinny. His anorak had a hood but not with fur on it and you could tell that he wasn't a girl because he had a moustache. He was definitely older than me and Angela, maybe nearly twenty. He had a plastic bag with bananas and a bottle and books. I could see the shapes.

We just stayed still and watched as he put down the bag and took off his anorak. Underneath he had a long woolly jumper with diamond designs on it and his jeans were really tight so his legs looked like sticks. He had a pair of runners on. They were dirty.

'I'm wringing wet,' he said, taking off the jumper. You could smell the sweat off him.

Angela had been quiet through all this but now she jumped up and told him he could have the chair because he was after being out in the cold and rain. He didn't say anything, just sat down. This meant he was right beside me so I moved away. The smell was strong.

'Who's this?'

'John,' said Angela.

'What's he here for?' He was taking off his shoes and socks. There was a hole in one of his socks and you could see his big toe. His toenail was dirty. He didn't sound annoyed or anything. He just wanted to know why I was there. It didn't sound like he really cared one way or the other. In a way, he reminded me of my father when he got back from work after he'd done overtime and you could tell that he didn't want to be asked questions or talked to.

He took off his socks and dried his feet with an old towel he got from under the pile of stuff on the floor. Then he got the bottle out of the bag. It was a bottle of cider. He poured some into a mug and drank it down.

Angela said something and the two of them laughed but I wasn't paying any attention. I was actually thinking about the smell of my father's slippers. Sometimes the smell of dogs' feet reminded me of it but there was something about the smell of Tony's feet that really reminded me of it too.

Angela offered me the bottle of cider. I took it and poured some into my mug. Fizz came to the top but didn't overflow. I could actually hear it. I said thanks and then I offered around the cigarettes. The two of them took one. I felt more part of everything as I lit the match and lit their cigarettes.

'Tony used to live on the pig farm,' said Angela.

Tony said nothing. He was eating a banana and smoking his cigarette and drinking cider all at the same time. It was warm and now there was cigarette smoke all over the place.

Tony stood up and took off his vest. He was hairy on his stomach. A boy in my class was like that. I called him the wolf boy when I thought about him.

Tony put on the transistor. It was punk music and I didn't like it. Just somebody roaring and shouting and no tune. I could feel the drink burning my throat and stomach. I wanted to take my shirt off because it was so warm but I couldn't because I knew everyone would laugh. I thought about my mother at the tenants' meeting and wondered what she would think if she could see me now. She joked that I might need to get a bra.

The music kept coming out of the transistor and after a while Tony poured more cider into my mug. It went over the side and there was a little pool on the ground. I looked at his stomach when he was bending down. I think he saw me looking. He smiled at me and for the first time I thought that maybe he was a nice person. He definitely looked different to nearly everybody I knew and this was a good sign. I had a long list of things I could never tell anybody and this was just another one. Maybe being a writer was about writing down all the things I could never tell anybody, but then what was the point in writing the made-up story of the girls who went back in time?

Angela did a big yawn. 'I'm bored,' she said. 'Neither of you have anything to say for yourselves.' I heard the yawn rather than saw it because she was sitting on the other side of the hut now and it was a bit dark.

Tony started doing this jumping up and down dance. He was holding the torch in one hand and flashing it around. He tried to pour Angela a drink while he was dancing but he just poured it on her legs.

She said he was an eejit and stood up. He moved so he was right in front of her. He was dancing slow but the music was fast.

I belched and I could taste whisky.

Tony said something to Angela and she said something back. They were whispering. I felt a bit sick. The two of them were right in front of each other and they were quiet for a while. I couldn't really see what was happening and I didn't really care but I was sure they were kissing each other and saying things about me.

Then Angela said let's go. Tony didn't move. He had his hands against the wall on either side of her face so she was trapped.

She said get out of my way but he still didn't move.

He had hair on his back too, the bottom part, and his skin was orange from the fire. He had the bottle of cider in one of his fists.

Then she shouted let me go and this time he moved. I

saw his face when he turned around and his eyes were like he was dying and you could only see the whites.

'Come on,' said Angela, 'we're going.'

I felt funny when I stood up. I could smell Tony. I could see my father's slippers in my mind's eye. They were brown and the smooth rubbery part of the heel was worn down so you could see the spongy stuff inside it.

Angela already had her anorak on. I put mine on too. Then we went out the door. Tony shouted at us to fuck off and then the door slammed behind us and there was loads of banging from inside the hut. The rain had stopped but it was freezing cold. We had our hoods up all the way home and we didn't talk much. I could only see a third of what I usually saw. I kept thinking about Tony, wondering if he slept in the hut, on the floor, in a sleeping bag by himself.

We walked fast and when we got back my mother was still out. Angela phoned her house to get a lift home from her father.

He came in the car and beeped to say he was there. We were watching telly. We still weren't talking very much but it was ok. I went to the door with her and said goodbye. I couldn't really see her father in the car and I wondered if maybe it was her mother this time. Her mother definitely looked like she could drive cars. My mother looked like she got buses and walked.

I knew it was a lie about graves being six feet deep because I'd looked into my father's grave and it was the deepest, darkest hole I'd ever seen. Then when I looked back at all the people standing around, and my mother by herself at the front of them, I realised none of them knew how deep the hole was, they couldn't have, not one of them, not even my mother. And I knew that none of them wanted me to tell them how deep that hole was. You could see it in their faces.

Ok so I know everything is relative and maybe this hole was actually six feet deep in reality but this six feet was further down than, say, the height of a six foot wall was up. Like one day can last twice as long as another day and still be only twenty four hours. Maybe some peoples' lives were twice as long as normal lives. Maybe my father's life was like that. He was five foot seven in his stocking feet.

Sometimes I imagined him in his coffin, rotting in the dark and quiet, and maybe us putting the flowers on the grave above him or my mother washing the stone and moving her lips but not saying anything and how we could never speak to him again or him tell a joke. I didn't believe in the afterlife or anything. But then when I had my dream with him being in the house it was like there was some reason for the dream, like he wanted to tell me something. Maybe it was just to say hello, and that he missed me and my mother (and being alive in general). If I could change anything it would be to have my father shot out of a spaceship and him to be floating around in space instead of being under the ground and rotting.

It was lashing again and me and my mother were on our way to the grave and my penis and testicles were itchy. I didn't know what to do about this so I prayed it would just go away. Sometimes I worried that my father could actually see me masturbating now that he was dead so I did believe in the afterlife really I suppose.

While we were waiting for the bus my mother announced that somebody at the tenants' association had told her about Angela's sister being missing.

I think she thought it wasn't right that neither me nor Angela had said anything to her even though we obviously knew. I could feel her looking at me funny.

The bus came and we got on and my mother paid our fares. One of the conductors who was usually on the buses had got run over, but not actually killed, and my mother talked to the new bus conductor about it. She didn't mention that my father had actually got run over too and I thought this was the same kind of forgetting that made me not tell her about Angela's sister disappearing.

Once my mother told me that when she was young she saw a little girl get run over by a bus and the girl's eyes came shooting out of her head and then they were hanging there on stalks that went back into her brain and there was blood gushing everywhere and the little girl was screaming and crying in agony and then she died. I thought of this little girl a lot since my father died but I never told my mother this. I knew she didn't like it when I thought too much about my father getting run over on the bike. But that little girl roaring and crying and her eyes on stalks and blood pouring all over her face was the reason why I thought about my father being a big tree trunk with all the leaves and branches gone and only one nail hammered into the side with only a little bit of blood coming out. I didn't want him to be too bad and blood everywhere. Not my father. I think that I will never see a poem lovely as a tree. Sometimes I said that to myself before I went asleep.

The bus filled up and my mother made me give up my seat to an old lady. It was actually better to stand than sit because my penis and testicles were itchy so I could scratch myself by putting my hand in my pocket and watch the street passing out the window. Everything was grey and everybody looked annoyed. I looked at my mother who was sitting there reading her book. She looked lonely. I tried to pretend I didn't know her, that she wasn't my mother, or that I was the ghost of her son watching her from beyond the grave. I really liked the part of her that was lonely on the bus reading because it was like me but then there was a part of her that was just not right, like she wished she wasn't my mother, and that part of her made me worry and not love her.

My father never wanted anything except for everybody to get on and he didn't really want to have a different family or a different son or a different wife, he just wanted peace and quiet so he could have a sleep on the weekends after he went to the pub or so he could watch the news.

My mother was nearly the same because she wanted everything to be alright as well but then she wanted everything to be brand new all the time and spick and span like she didn't want what she already had at all, as if as soon as you had a thing that you wanted then it was no good. So she always wanted new things or to paint things or to put up wallpaper. They argued a lot over wallpapering and painting and him going to the pub. When my father was alive my mother didn't read books so maybe that meant she was bored now or lonely or maybe she just had more time for herself. She was always putting Nivea on her face and Atrixo on her hands. Always in front of the dressing table mirror where I loved the smell.

We stopped at the hut outside the big gates. I liked buying plants for the grave but we didn't do it every time and this time was one of those. We did buy a packet of crisps for me and a packet of peanuts for her, and I remembered that I'd heard a thing on the radio about the smallest pub in the world and that it was just around the corner from the graveyard. I thought about saying to my mother that we should go there afterwards but I decided not to because she didn't like pubs. My father did. He always looked happy in the pub. My mother always looked like she was waiting to go home when we were in the pub, so she could cook the dinner or something.

What I remembered about the actual day of the funeral was how everybody looked like they didn't know what to do or where to go. We walked to the grave and I didn't even know where it was and the others didn't either but we got there because somebody must have checked. I remember thinking the crowd is snaking to the grave. Snaking was a good word for that day.

My mother was all in black and roaring and crying and people kept saying her name, people who didn't usually say her name, and my mother's secret name was Madame X that day, and only I knew that, and I knew it because Madame X was the name of a film we'd watched together on the night my father died and it had a really sad ending. I knew this was a sad ending happening to us now with the father dead in the coffin. I was glad that people didn't know my mother's secret name on the day of the funeral. They were getting my mother's name wrong on the day of my father's funeral and they didn't know it.

I wanted them all to leave me alone with Madame X.

But my mother wasn't Madame X anymore. Now she was just my mother. She didn't even have her polka dot dress on. We were just people going to see a grave with a skeleton in it.

Another reason why I didn't like going to the grave was because I kept thinking I was supposed to be sad when I was there and I actually wasn't. People who were alive made me sadder than dead people, like when I looked into the back windows of the houses and wondered what everybody was doing and if they were lonely or when Angela looked at the empty gardens and felt depressed because people weren't in them. It was the same thing as when you shoot a garda and it's supposed to be really bad but it's part of a garda's job to get shot so what's the problem? Dead people are dead and gone so don't worry about them. I want to be thrown on the scrapheap when I'm dead or dumped in the sea off a cliff or shot into space or just burnt like a Viking on his boat. Anyway, I still had my dream about my father coming to see us in the house and everything being ok. That's how I remembered him. It was nothing to do with the grave and his skeleton rotting in the dark coffin under the ground.

A big beam of light came out of the clouds and all the birds started singing all of a sudden.

We passed a family who looked sad. A father and a girl and a boy. Maybe the mother was dead. I really, really didn't want my mother to die because there would be another funeral and the same people. Maybe I would call myself Orphan X and talk to nobody. Or son of the deceased Madame and Monsieur X. Or just plain X.

When we got to the grave there was the awkward bit always at the start where I didn't really know what to do and my mother stood there holding her hands in front and moving her lips with her eyes closed. As usual I stood there looking at her and wanting her to stop and then looking at the headstone which I actually liked because me and my mother had picked it. It was a kind of reddish brown, all smooth with shiny black flecks and it had gold letters on it saying his name and when he was born and died and that he was missed by me and my mother. Sometimes when I was in bed I'd think of the stone there in the dark in the middle of the graveyard and that would make me feel ok.

After the praying, my mother would get to work with

her little shovel that she had in her handbag and the little bottle of water and the J-cloth. She'd make it all clean and get rid of weeds etc. and I'd help and then wander around and look at other graves and she'd pray more. Under my breath I would say to my father that I was waiting for my next dream with him in it but I didn't do any praying and I never moved my lips when I was speaking under my breath. After she was finished, my mother would have her packet of peanuts and I would have my packet of cheese and onion and we'd have a cup of tea out of the flask.

Everything happened like this again this day except when I looked at my mother after she had got rid of the weeds and wiped the stone with the J cloth, there was a tear in her eye. Actually, it had come out of her eye and was rolling down her cheek when I saw it. And she saw me seeing it and she wiped it away and I said are you alright, mam? and she said she was fine and smiled and sucked air into her nose. It was the first time since the funeral that I'd seen a tear roll down her cheek when we were at the grave. I wanted the tear to fall off and land on a slug and turn it into mush.

'I'm not crying because I'm sad,' she said.

'Then why are you crying?'

'I miss him, son, but I'm crying because I miss him less than I used to.'

'That sounds like you're sad,' I said.

Her eyes were watering but she was smiling. One of the tears rolled down her cheek and fell off but it went on her dress and didn't make it to the ground. The dress was plain navy blue. You could see the wet patch on where it stuck out for her breasts.

'Are you finished your tea?'

I said yes.

She poured the bottom of her cup onto the grave.

'A drop of tea for your poor father.'

'He won't like it without the sugar,' I said.

'Maybe he's given up sugar now that he's in heaven,' she said, screwing the top on the flask.

She looked up at the sky so I did too. There was no heavenly beam anymore.

'At least the rain stayed away,' she said.

That night we got on really well, a bit like it was in the year after my father died, when it was just the two of us at home every night reading and watching television. We had a fry for tea and I ate it all. Usually I threw some of every fry out, mostly the black pudding and the tomatoes. It was easy to trick my mother because she was always going to the cooker or going to put the kettle on or getting something out of the fridge and you could just put the food in a bit of toilet roll in your pocket or something. Anyway, this time I ate it all, every bit. My mother thought that fried tomatoes were my father's favourite food but I thought it was roast beef. We hadn't had roast beef in ages, it was always roast chicken these days.

'Maybe we'll have roast beef next week,' she said.

I said I thought that was a good idea.

◆

Sunday came around again. I did my exercises in the bedroom with the Gloria Gaynor. Then we went to mass. No matter how hard I tried (and I didn't try that hard anymore) I couldn't find a reason for going to mass. Priests got on my nerves. Sometimes I actually hated them. We had a Bible with coloured pictures when I was in primary school and one of the pictures was of all these boys who'd had their fingers cut off because they wouldn't say they didn't believe in God or something. They were all lying around this room roaring and crying in their togas which were like mini-skirts really and they had blood coming out of their hands and you could see fingers all over the floor. Their faces were holy. I couldn't imagine the priests who said mass letting their fingers be cut off for anything.

My mother actually liked some of the priests. She had favourite ones and she'd get annoyed if one she didn't like said the mass instead of one she liked. The worst one had hair growing up the back of his neck. A wolf-priest. He roamed around Clonduff every full moon. Once I saw him in the garden in the middle of the night, howling and growling at the moon. He caught me looking out the window and he hopped on top of the coal-shed and legged it down the back alley between the houses and he was gone. He knew I knew. He'd be looking straight at me when he was giving out and saying you'll all go to hell or whatever he said when he was doing his sermons.

The priests all lived in a prefab on the side of Clonduff Park and the church was another prefab around near the shops. They were going to build a proper church at some stage and they had a collection for it every week. The men who did the collection all sat at the back during the mass. They would have been my father's friends if he was alive and actually lived in Clonduff with us. I didn't really like the look of them. Except for one. He had a big black beard and glasses and a big nose. There was just something about him that made me think he would have been a good friend for my father. I never spoke to him or anything. I caught his eye a few times but he didn't seem to care.

On the way home we got the paper. Dear Valerie said to wait until you were twenty-seven before you told the world you were bisexual because usually it was only a phase. I thought about gladiators a lot. But I was trying not to think about them because my penis and testicles were all red and itchy from the ointment I'd put on to see what it felt like. Now I had to think about going to the doctors but I knew I couldn't go to the doctor my mother went to, and that was the only doctor I knew.

We had our dinner when we got back and then I got the bike out. I had to put new brakes on and oil it. Fixing the bike was something my father taught me to do. I did it in the back garden and my mother read the papers inside in front of the fire.

It was cold but it wasn't raining and the sky was blue. It was nice to be fixing the bike. Sometimes I looked up at the sky. I liked looking from the big to the small. There was a little tree in the garden next door and birds were hopping in and out of it. The family next door were shouting and screaming at each other and the birds were chirping in the tree. I'd look from the tree to the screw I was screwing in, or the brake-pad I was straightening, and my hands were covered in black dirt. From the sky to the tree to the screw. It made me happy.

Angela turned up in the middle of all this. I didn't hear her come in but when I went into the house to get a drink of water, there she was talking to my mother. They were looking at each other funny and Angela had a polka dot blouse on and my mother had a polka dot dress on.

Men couldn't wear polka dots. My father wore brown or grey or black or navy or beige clothes with white or blue shirts and white vest and underpants. He was buried in his coffin in a pinstripe suit. Black with a grey pinstripe. He had a white shirt. I wanted to be buried in a toga. The word for shirt and the word for skirt are nearly the same but the difference is huge between them. It is the difference between a pinstripe and a polka dot. It is the difference between a penis and a vagina.

'Your poor mam,' my mother was saying, 'she must be in an awful state.'

'My dad is too,' said Angela.

I drank a big glass of water down. It had no taste and yet I could actually taste it.

I left them there and went back into the garden and turned the bike the right way up. I scratched the back of my hand on the pebbledash. A plane was roaring across the sky and I imagined it crashing and exploding and everybody on board screaming and crying. Then I heard Angela's voice calling my name from above. Her head was sticking out my bedroom window. A big purple cloud was floating over the house. The world went dark.

'Come up here!' She was whispering out loud, waving a cigarette at me. 'Look what I've got!'

Big plops of rain started and there was a growl of thunder far away. A damp smell came out of the muck and the ground and the bricks and the coal. It actually followed me into the house and up the stairs.

The cigarette was nearly gone but I had a drag anyway. It made me cough and Angela started laughing and doing impressions of me coughing and we broke our hearts for a while. I even thought for a second that we were going to kiss each other but that thought went away. In a way, it was like Angela wasn't a girl or, maybe, it was that I didn't feel like a boy around her. Nothing made sense and everything got mixed up with the two of us.

There was more thunder outside.

My mother shouted up the stairs that I was to close the windows.

'Marion's afraid of thunder,' said Angela, 'but I like it.'

I asked her what else Marion was afraid of. The question was just inside my head and then it was out.

Angela was sitting on the bed and she leaned back now so she was actually lying on her back looking at the ceiling. I could see up her skirt but she had tights on.

'She's afraid of my Dad,' she said, and her voice sounded kind of sleepy. 'They argue all the time but the thing is he lets her away with things he wouldn't let me away with.'

'Like what?'

'Like make-up and mini skirts.' She sat up. 'This skirt is hers.'

She rubbed the skirt like she was brushing crumbs off. It was a kind of purpley grey colour, like the cloud in the sky, or the roses on a boy's birthday cake.

'She'd kill me if she knew I was wearing it.'

'I hope she's not afraid now,' I said.

'What do you mean?'

'I just hope Marion's ok, wherever she is,' I said.

We went quiet for approximately sixty seconds. We were both thinking, I suppose. Then I said: 'She used to go out with Tony in the workman's hut, didn't she?'

'Yeah.'

'And Tony knows Paul the Rapist?'

There was so much stuff that Angela just thought was normal that I thought was unusual or that hadn't happened to me or I hadn't really thought about before.

'Who's Paul the Rapist?' Angela looked a bit confused.

'Paul who goes out with Pauline,' I said. 'I call him Paul the Rapist because of what he did to you.'

In my head, the rape of Angela was connected with the disappearance of Marion. I wasn't sure what the connection was except that two sisters getting into so much trouble made me think they were asking for trouble, like they were sluts or something. But Angela didn't actually look like a slut.

'Paul didn't really rape me,' she said, 'not in a bad way. We had a fight, that's all. We weren't really going with each other. He'd been going with Marion and she dumped him for Tony.'

'So Marion went out with Paul and Tony?'

Angela looked at me. She looked straight into my eyes. 'The thing is,' she said.

But she didn't say anything else and approximately six seconds passed.

'The thing is what?' I said.

I was beginning to feel really annoyed but then, really fast, all in one breath she said:

'The thing is all this happened in this house downstairs in the kitchen.'

'All what happened?'

'We used to hang around in these houses before they put the doors on, me and Marion and Paul and Tony.'

'You're messing.'

'I'm not. I just didn't know whether to tell you.'

'Why wouldn't you tell me?'

'Something weird happened here, that's why.'

She went to the window and lit a cigarette. She had a drag and passed it to me. She was looking straight into my eyes again. I was looking straight back. Smoke was coming out of her nose.

'Do you believe in ghosts?' she said.

I took a drag on the cigarette, right down inside of me, down into my stomach. We were looking so hard at each other, I was wondering if we could read each other's minds. You see, I had seen a ghost. Not actually in the house but down near the phonebox on the estate. He was dressed in a grey raincoat. He didn't say anything. He just sort of stared at me when I was walking past. It was a bit like he wanted to tell me something. It was just after we moved to Clonduff. I was coming back from the library. The next week I saw that where he was standing was actually a ditch so he couldn't have actually been standing there. He must have been just floating or hovering. I thought that maybe he was killed on that spot or something. But he didn't seem evil or scary, just lonely and sad. I didn't believe in really scary dead ghosts. Sometimes I wondered if my father haunted the road where he was killed but I didn't really think he did. I'd never seen him there when I went back.

'JOHN?' My mother's voice was suddenly coming up the stairs.

I put the cigarette out quickly and me and Angela flapped our hands around to get the smoke out the window. The rain was coming down hard and the wind was blowing through the house. She poked her head into my room: 'Close that window! There's an awful draft!'

I said ok and tried to look like we hadn't been smoking and off she went back downstairs.

The interruption kind of broke the spell of ghosts and

weird things happening that me and Angela were in the middle of.

'I made you a Bowie tape but I forgot to bring it,' she said, changing the subject altogether. But I wasn't going to let that subject be changed, no sirree.

'What is the weird thing that happened in this house, Angela?'

I was lying on the floor now and she was sitting on the bed. She made her eyes go up and around, as if I was forcing her to tell me a secret, as if it wasn't her who started all this.

'We had a séance here. That's all. Down in the kitchen. We contacted a lady who lived in Clonduff House years ago. She told us the wrong person got blamed for killing her.'

The rain was lashing down on the window.

'Who was at this séance?'

'Me and Marion and Tony.'

'Where was Paul the Rapist?'

'He'd gone off because of the row.'

'What row?'

'I had a row with him because I wouldn't...'

'Because you wouldn't what?'

She made a hole with her thumb and another finger and stuck a finger from her other hand through the hole. It meant sex. I'd seen boys do it at school but it was funny seeing Angela do it because she'd never been shy about saying sex before this.

This time it was me who made my eyes go up and around: 'Just say it, Angela.'

She looked at me, and I wondered if she was going to cry:

'Because I wouldn't let him have sex with me.'

Approximately ten seconds passed.

'So Tony Byrne from the workman's hut?' I was trying to get everything straight in my head. 'Tony was at a séance here in my house, in this house, and you never bothered to tell me before now?'

'There weren't even doors then,' she said.

I was still lying on the floor. I put my face right on the carpet so that the carpet was like a whole world stretching away from me into the distance. There was a spider walking along under the bed. I wondered if it was the same spider that I'd seen the other day, the one I'd hit with my slipper, or maybe even a relative of that spider. I thought of all the spiders in my father's coffin and how his skeleton was like a whole world to them, or like in *Alien* when they find the huge body with its stomach split open on the planet with the eggs. I thought all this for approximately ninety seconds.

'The rain is stopped.' It was Angela again.

I didn't want to go out anymore. I didn't look up. I kept

looking under the bed. I couldn't see the spider but I thought he was probably watching me from somewhere in there in the dark.

The truth was I was hurt that Angela had told me none of this before now, more hurt than I wanted to be. In my stomach I had a feeling that was bad and full of worry.

Angela got up and put on the Kate Bush.

She said why don't we have another cigarette and I said yes. I didn't want to look like I was sulking.

First I went to the toilet and scratched my penis and testicles. It was still red down there so I put more talc on. Then I washed my hands in hot water. I felt better when I came out and Angela and me were nearly back to normal so that was good and the cigarette didn't make me cough but we decided not to go out on our bikes anyway because it was cold.

While we were smoking, the phone went and I could hear my mother talking to somebody and then she called Angela to the phone.

Angela came back in approximately four minutes and said her mother was coming to pick her up.

'Mam sounded like something was wrong,' she said. 'But there's always something wrong these days.'

We listened to the music and wrote down notes for our novel but we didn't get much done. My heart wasn't in it and I kept thinking about what Angela had told me about the séance and everything. Angela looked like she had things on her mind as well. When her mother came and knocked, my mother spoke to her for a little while. Angela didn't know this but my mother was talking low and using her special serious voice so we couldn't hear what they were saying. Anyway after approximately three minutes they called Angela down.

I followed and helped to put the bike in the boot of the car.

When they were gone, I went back upstairs and did my exercises without even listening to music. My mother was down watching telly but I stayed upstairs. I lay under the bed for approximately seventeen minutes pretending to be dead, thinking about my father in his grave and all the quiet and darkness around him, then I read my book.

My mother called me when the news was on because there was a thing about Angela's sister being missing but I didn't get down on time to see it. She said that Angela's parents were interviewed and they were very upset. She asked me if Angela had ever said anything that made me think she knew something about where Marion actually was.

I pretended not to know what she meant and she got annoyed and said I knew exactly what she meant and I was just being awkward and then she asked me again and I got annoyed and shouted at her that I didn't know anything and I'd never met Marion.

She said she was only asking and then went all quiet and we didn't really speak to each other for the rest of the night.

I didn't do my homework, I just read my book. I was starving when I went to bed so I sneaked into the kitchen when the house was dark and made a Slender and drank it down really quick but then I ate loads of biscuits too and I felt a bit sick.

That night I dreamed that my father came into the room. There was no door for him to open, just a hole in the wall and he was a mixture between an alien and a vampire but not evil. He sat by my bed where there isn't a chair in real life but in the dream there was a kind of a throne that had space age controls and it was floating. He said that he was fine, that he was looking after me and my mother. He pressed a button in the arm of the throne and his stomach opened like a spaceship and I could see a little baby with huge, big eyes inside in a kind of a cage.

He said that sometimes bad things happen to babies but that he was minding this baby and that this baby was actually me. He didn't say anything else and that was the end of the dream as far as I remember but when I woke up I knew that my father was looking after me and my mother and that everything would be alright, it would just take a while.

◆

But then the week got off to a bad start. It was raining again all day Monday and I hadn't done the essay I was supposed to do and the teacher gave me a note to give to my mother asking her to come in and talk about my school work. I gave it to her as soon as I got home knowing that there would be an almighty row.

There was.

I told her the truth, that I didn't care about school anymore, that I liked nobody there and that nobody liked me. I shouted this at her. I stood at one side of the kitchen and she stood at the other and I shouted at her and she started crying so I stopped but when I said I was sorry she started shouting at me so I went upstairs and slammed the door and left her down there.

It was freezing cold so I got under the covers and read my book with my torch but I couldn't concentrate. In the end I had to go downstairs because I was starving but we didn't talk to each other. I had a ham sandwich and a glass of water and a packet of cheese and onion. I worried all night about the rash on my penis and testicles so I hardly slept and I didn't have any dreams. I did pray to my father and told him I was sorry for the row with my mother and that I would make it up to her. He said it was alright and that people often had rows when they loved each other.

To be honest, I already knew this anyway because, about a year before he got killed, me and my father had loads of rows. He started saying to me that I needed to go out more and play sports. He liked football and I didn't and I think he thought that it was bad that I didn't have friends. I was always good at school then but the school started taking PE and football really seriously like they were real subjects and they told my mother and father that I needed to get better at sport. He tried to get me to go to the park and actually play football a few times but I didn't want to and then he just started picking on me all the time. We used to go for walks in the park on weekends and then we'd go to the pub and I'd have a coke and a packet of cheese and onion but I even stopped wanting to do that. Then I heard him and my mother arguing about me, and him saying to her that she was turning me into a girl, and so I just stopped talking to him altogether for about two weeks.

Then one day, he came into my room and sat on the bed and asked me if there was anything wrong. I said no, nothing, but he said he knew there was something wrong and I started crying and I said I'd heard him say

I was like a girl. Right away he gave me a big hug and he said he knew I wasn't a girl but he was just worried about me and he was really sorry. He said I was a real boy. And then we went for a walk to the pub and he let me have a mouthful of Guinness.

The funny thing was, as I said previously, I never knew what a boy was actually supposed to be like and I still don't. Even now at school I watch them running around, and sometimes I'm running around too, but always it's a bit like I'm pretending to know the rules to a weird game I don't actually know how to play.

Maybe the thing about Angela was being her friend made me feel like I wasn't pretending. And maybe that was why I never completely stopped thinking about kissing her even though I didn't actually want to and my penis didn't actually get hard.

Anyway, about my father, things did get back to normal after that weird time and it was just after then when he bought me the bike for my birthday. It was the biggest present I ever had in my life and that definitely felt like he was saying sorry.

But all of that was ages and ages ago, and now it was just me and my mother, and the rain and everything, and us not really getting on because of the note from the school, and me feeling a bit weird around Angela because she hadn't told me about the séance, and on top of that there was the problem of my penis and testicles so, well, I suppose I was feeling a bit depressed.

During the week I had to go to the credit union for my mother (I knew it would be the beginning of me and her talking to each other again if I went without complaining) and anyway I wanted to go to the library and look for books about what it was like to actually live and work in Hollywood. So after I got back from school this day and had my dinner I got the bike out and off I went. I knew everything was going to get a bit easier between me and my mother because when she was saying goodbye she was all smiles.

It was freezing out and pitch black because the lights on the roads around the estate weren't on for some reason but it had stopped raining and, once I got going, it was a good cycle and you soon warm up on the bike anyway. I sang Kate Bush until I got to the village and everything was normal with normal lights and people and traffic. The library was in the Greenlawn Shopping Centre, over the chip shop, next door to the chemist, next door to the credit union. I locked my bike to the railings around the car park and went into the credit union and paid the money. Then I went to the library.

Libraries for me were the same thing as churches for my mother. The first time I read a really good book was like finding a pot of gold inside my own bedroom. The book was about children who find treasure inside a cave on an island. Every night around the time when I was reading this book I used to fall asleep and dream that I was floating down a long cave and there were treasure chests with jewels and golden crowns and pearl brooches and tiaras all around the place. Two children were exploring this cave but I couldn't tell if they were boys or girls even though I was one of them. In a way, I was both of them. They'd find a box with a head inside in it, sometimes it was a nun's head and sometimes it was a priest's. The head would start screaming and shouting and then I'd wake up.

I handed over the books I had and went looking around the shelves for new ones. I went to the cinema section first but there wasn't anything about normal people in Hollywood so I just got a book about science fiction films. Then I went looking for a James Herbert and I got one called The Fog. Then I got Nineteen Eighty Four because the David Bowie album was based on it.

They flashed the lights to let us know that we had to start thinking about leaving. There were big glass windows and when the lights flashed you could see down on the car park and the road and it felt a little bit like we were in a spaceship or something and we were just floating over the world reading our books in the quiet for ever and ever. The man behind the desk was weird looking and all his skin was red and flaky like he had dandruff of the face. I actually had dandruff on my eyebrows once but it didn't spread. Now I had this rash that wouldn't go away on my penis and testicles. I was tired of thinking about my penis and testicles so I decided to just say Down Under in future, like my penis and testicles were actually in Australia.

Anyway, I got back on my bike and started cycling home. It was drizzling rain but I was in a good mood for the first time that week so I didn't mind. But when I got out of the park that led into the estate there was a gang of lads at the beginning of Clonduff Grove. They were all standing around watching a fight and I stopped because I was afraid they would pick on me if I went through.

None of them was really paying any attention to me because of the fight so I was able to watch for approximately thirty seconds. One of them was shouting, 'Go on, Paul, fucking smash his head in.' Then they all started chanting something.

It was definitely Paul the Rapist doing the kicking. I was nearly sure of it. Angela had said he was trouble.

I would have had to cycle right past them all to get to my house and I knew that could be a problem so I decided to go right around the back of the estate and come in that way. But when I got there another gang of lads was roaring and shouting at each other and playing football and I didn't like the look of them either. I stopped for a second to figure out what to do and then a stone whizzed past my ear. It was time to move. Sometimes Clonduff was a hard place to get around and this was one of those times.

I cycled back down the back road and I was just coming to the turn, not paying any attention really, just looking at the backs of the houses and all the lights on in the bedrooms and then I must have gone over some glass because I could suddenly feel the road was bumpy and I had a puncture.

I pulled the brakes and the bike made a weird whining sound and stopped by one of the big orange lights. It was flashing on and off. Cars whizzed past and it started to really lash. I looked around and everything was dark and miserable and the rain was bucketing down.

And that was when I saw him. The same one I'd seen before. He was hovering over the grass by the side wall of the estate. It took me a while to be sure he was there because he was in a funny place where you wouldn't expect to see anyone.

I wasn't scared but I didn't really like the way he was just staring at me and the wolves were howling in the fields and the moon came out from behind a purple cloud and in the yellowy light I saw his face and it was a screaming skull, and that was a sign for me to get moving. I didn't panic. I kept my eye on him and he kept his eye on me and I dropped the bike by the lamp post without taking my eye off him. In a way, I felt sad for him out there in the rain without a home to go to. Then he suddenly started floating towards me like a proper ghost and that was when I legged it.

I grabbed my library books off the carrier and dashed across the road as fast as I could. I was soaked but I just kept going and I didn't look back. I headed toward the new houses where there was no lights and no doors on the insides. I wasn't sure I could remember how to get there but Tony's hut was in the back garden of one of these and there was a heater and a torch and I would be inside.

I tripped over because the ground was bumpy and slippy and I wished Angela was there because she would know where to go but I got up and kept going and it was really lashing it down and I found the row of empty houses like dead whales at the bottom of the sea and I got to the last one and threw myself at the door and it opened right away and I ran through and there was stuff written on the walls but I couldn't see what it was and I ran through the back door and into the garden and the black hut like a space ship was there and I ran up to it and banged on the door and shouted LET ME IN! LET ME IN! and the door opened and the door opened and someone stuck a torch in my face.

'What do you want?'

'It's John,' I said. 'I was here with Angela the other day.'

The torch got pointed at the floor and I could see the shape of Tony.

'Can I come in out of the rain?' I sounded like a girl.

The torch came in my face again, and I could feel him looking at me for approximately five seconds, then he moved the torch beam down to the ground and made a funny move with his head and opened the door more and I took that as a sign to go in, so in I went.

There was a stool beside the superser and I sat down.

He closed the door and put the bolt across. I was thinking *you are my saviour.* There was punk music on the transistor. You could hear the rain hitting the sides of the hut.

'Bad night out there,' he said, putting the torch facing upward on the table. The light made his face look unusual. He sat on the table, picked up the James Herbert I got from the library and brushed some raindrops off its plastic cover. He dangled his legs. He was in his stocking feet.

I told him Angela had said to read it (i.e. the James Herbert).

'Looks good,' he said.

Then we said nothing for approximately forty five seconds except he offered me a cigarette but I didn't take it and then I took off my jacket and hung it on the stool in front of the fire. The air in the hut was warm from the superser and you could smell my father's slippers and you could hear the rain lashing down outside and the punk music playing.

'So, what are you doing out in this weather?' he said, looking at me funny.

'I was on the bike,' I said.

We were quiet for approximately fifteen seconds.

'I got a puncture,' I said.

He didn't look like he heard me. He was looking at my other library book.

'Angela tells me you're going to be a writer,' he said, looking up from the book.

I said yeah.

'So what are you going to write about?'

This was a hard question but I knew that he expected a good answer, that he wouldn't ever take me seriously if I sounded like I was stupid and hadn't thought about this before.

'I don't really know yet,' I said. 'I want it to be exciting. Maybe horror stories. Or whodunnits. Not just I did this, I did that. Not boring. I want to write about things people are scared to talk about.'

My voice stopped and there was only the transistor and even the rain had stopped. I felt like the workman's hut was the whole world and we were all alone in it, and like I didn't know anything, like I was pretending everything, and I was thick and he could see through me, right down into my soul.

Suddenly the light from the torch went out but it wasn't actually pitch black and I could still see his face.

'You need to write if you want to be a writer,' he said, looking a bit pleased with himself, as if he'd said something really intelligent.

I actually thought it was a bit obvious that you had to write to be a writer but I didn't say anything right then because I was enjoying being there, looking at his face in the faint glow from the superser. And anyway, now that he'd said something that I thought was a bit stupid I was thinking that maybe I wasn't the worst in the world. Maybe he was stupid too. Maybe everybody was.

He struck a match and lit a candle and the light changed. He made some wax drop on this stone that was kind of shaped like a skull, then he stood the candle on top of it.

Once my father told me that I wasn't to hide my light under a bushel and I didn't really know what it meant and then I never got a chance to ask him but maybe this was it now. Maybe knowing that Tony and me were sort of the same was part of it. Maybe our two faces floating around in the dark was part of it. Maybe everything was part of it and, even though I wasn't actually sure what a bushel was, maybe my light was out from under it.

The skull with the candle stuck on it kind of smiled at me and I took this as a sign that everything was more or less alright. Maybe the ghost on the road would smile if you gave him a chance.

'Do you believe in ghosts?' I was asking Tony but I was looking at the skull.

'Ghosts? Nah.'

'I do,' I said. 'I came here because I was running away from one. He was floating around on the road. I think I saw him before too. I'm not scared of him or anything.'

'Then why were you running away from him?'

'I think I was scared of him when I was running but now I'm not.' I was only beginning to understand this.

'That doesn't make sense.' He belched and then he laughed a little bit to himself.

'I know what I mean,' I said. And that was true. 'Anyway, I know you believe in ghosts because I know you were at the séance with Angela before I moved into my house.'

He made his eyes go up and around: 'That Angela has a great imagination.'

He started fiddling around in the pile of stuff on the floor in the corner. Something told me that the cigarette in his hand was really a joint. I'd never actually seen one in real life before then but the smell was definitely different to cigarettes, and this was longer and skinnier than any cigarette I'd seen. I noticed that he had an earring too and I wondered how much it hurt when they stuck the pin thing in you for the first time, and I thought about how earrings used to be only for girls and now boys had them too, and while I was thinking all this and watching him I noticed for the first time that there was something new about the hut too. There was a different type of floor. Before, it was just one dark colour, I was sure of it. Now there was a design of black and white squares like on a game of chess. I tried to imagine my house with black and white squares everywhere. My mother wouldn't like it. Then I imagined it with no doors and Angela and Tony and Marion doing the séance and the glass moving around and saying something terrible was going to happen and in this séance I could see, clear as day, that Angela, Tony and Marion were in trouble and somewhere down the line they were going to find a nun or priest's head in a box or go into a room where it was raining liver and kidneys and the devil was dancing with an old lady and she'd be roaring and laughing, covered in blood. And then I knew that something bad had happened to Marion, and Angela and Tony knew what it was and were afraid to say what it was. Maybe they'd already found the box with the nun or priest's head in it. Maybe that's what the ghost was trying to tell me. He wasn't a scary ghost. He was trying to warn me. Maybe he was actually a friend of my father's.

Tony's voice brought me back to earth: 'I knew I had batteries somewhere.'

He'd put batteries in the torch while I was thinking through all this and now everything was a bit more normal with the torch on. He reached over to hand me the joint but I said no. I could see it was all soggy where his spit had got on it.

'Anyway, just because I was at a séance doesn't mean I believe in ghosts.' He smiled. 'I only did it to give Marion a scare.'

It was the first time I'd heard him say Marion's name and it made me feel a bit weird or something, maybe because he actually used to go out with her and now she was gone and I'd never met her so being here and hearing Tony talk about her made her seem more real or something.

I asked him if he knew where she was.

'Why would I know where she is? I don't care if I never see that girl again.'

'Why?'

'She gave me VD. That's why.'

As I said previously, I'd never met anyone with VD

before, and now with the rash Down Under and everything, I felt it was lucky to meet somebody who was so open about having it. I could maybe get some advice as to what to do about the rash. But still and all, the thought of Marion, Angela's sister, having VD was wrong or something. I just didn't believe it. Maybe it was because she was a girl. Or maybe it was because I couldn't imagine Angela ever having VD and Marion, in a way, was like the same person.

'I actually think I have VD,' I said.

'You?' He shone the torch straight in my face. 'Who've you been at it with?'

'Nobody.'

'Then you don't have VD, unless it's the bloody Immaculate Infection.'

He started laughing, but not really loud.

I felt awkward but I laughed too anyway. I didn't make many laughing noises though. Just a big smile and moved my head around a bit.

When he stopped laughing, I stopped too. I could feel him looking at me but I could only sort of see his face through the torch beam.

'Have you ever even had sex?'

I did think about pretending that I had but I knew he'd see through me so I said no.

He turned the torch off: 'Well, you have to have sex

before you get VD because that's how it gets spread.'

I told him about the rash Down Under and he said if I hadn't had sex it wasn't VD and to go to the doctor and get ointment and it would go away.

He called me a weirdo but his voice was kind, and I tried to remember what colour his eyes were but I couldn't. I decided I'd have a look when I was going.

The station on the transistor was just crackle now. He picked it up and fiddled around with the buttons. Different voices and music and funny sounds kept coming and going. Then he turned it off.

'The reception is shite down here.' He threw the transistor into the pile of stuff in the corner.

'Why didn't you stay up in the caravan?' I said.

He didn't say anything for approximately ten seconds, just looked at the squares on the floor, then:

'There was trouble between me and the lad Marion used to go out with, and the farmer died. It was a bad situation.'

'What did the farmer die of?'

'I don't know, a broken heart, I suppose.'

I'd heard of people dying of broken hearts but I didn't really know how it could happen because your heart was actually fine but you died anyway. You died of sadness. Like the monkeys who were kept in cages by themselves.

'Did his wife die on him?'

'No, it was his brother who died on him,' he said. 'They lived on that farm all their lives.'

'How could you die of a broken heart over your own brother?'

He didn't answer and I started to feel stupid again. He didn't mean the farmers were queers. At least I didn't think he did. Usually when anybody said anything about queers there was a special laugh or joke about it and Tony wasn't laughing or joking. But then what did he mean? For some reason I started to get a bit scared. This was a feeling in my stomach.

'What was the trouble?' I said.

'What trouble?'

'Between you and Marion's boyfriend.'

'You're full of questions.'

'It's a writer's job.'

He smiled. 'Me and Paul had a row over Marion. We wrecked the gaff.'

'Paul who raped Angela?'

'Did Angela tell you that?'

I looked at him with a look that said yes, she told me, as if we both knew that Angela was mad and always telling lies. He made his eyes go up and around.

'Be careful with that one,' he said. 'She's trouble.'

We just sat there then for approximately ninety seconds,

maybe even longer, without saying anything. He was making funny faces and I got the impression that he didn't mean for me to see them.

Eventually I just said, 'anyway, I better go. The rain is stopped.'

I stood up but he didn't move. I put my jacket on even though it was still wet. I wanted him to stand up and say goodbye or something but he seemed lost in thought. He was just turning the torch off and on and staring at the circle it made on the ceiling. I wasn't going to see the colour of his eyes this time.

'Don't say anything to Angela about Marion having VD or I'll kill you,' he said.

I said I wouldn't, then I said goodbye but he didn't say anything else so I grabbed my books and off I went. Once I was outside it was like I'd never really been there at all. The black outside of the hut made it look like just a piece of the dark, like I'd stepped out of a piece of black air.

When I got to the main road I saw that the ghost man was waiting for me, hovering over my bike, slightly to the left, under the orange light. I wasn't afraid of him this time but I kept my eye on him and as I got closer he descended a bit. The light was flashing on and off and making a buzzing noise and it made his face look ancient, but it didn't look like an actual skull anymore.

The old grey mac he was wearing flapped in the wind.

'Have you got a match?' His voice was like any other old man's voice. Nothing particularly ghost-like.

I had matches in my pocket. They felt a bit damp but I held them up and he descended a bit more and took them. His hands were skinny and purple with horrible yellow nails but you couldn't see through them or anything. It took three goes but eventually he lit his cigarette. He handed me back the matches and ascended a bit.

I asked him if he knew where my father was.

'Your father is grand and he loves you and your mam,' he said.

'Why can't he come and be a ghost on earth and appear to me like the way you are?'

'I don't really know the answer to that.' He had a long drag on the cigarette and started coughing and it made him move backwards in little spurts like each cough was a jet engine going off and pushing him away.

I shouted after him, 'You're hopeless. You know nothing.'

He stopped coughing and came back to me really fast, almost like flying, but in a standing up position.

'I know that it's not your father that has the problem here,' he said. 'Your father is properly dead and gone and that's the way things are supposed to be. I'm the one who's stuck here.'

'In ClonduffSiberia,' I said, but I said it under my breath, only moving my lips.

The ghost was having another coughing fit.

'Are they real cigarettes or ghost ones?' I said.

'They're real enough.' He was kind of struggling for breath which seemed like an unusual thing for a ghost to do.

'Can I have one?'

He descended and held out the pack for me to take one but then he coughed as I was reaching out and I missed because he moved backwards a bit. But then he stopped coughing again and I got to take a cigarette from the box. They were the untipped ones like my father smoked. I said thanks. It took me three goes but I got it lit in the end. Then it was my turn to cough.

When I stopped coughing I asked him who he was.

'I don't know, son.' He sounded sad. 'I think my name is Flanagan. Or Brannigan. I'm not sure.'

We just stood there for approximately sixty seconds, smoking our cigarettes. He was kind of bobbing up and down. Eventually, I thought of asking him if he knew where Marion was.

'Who's Marion?'

'A girl who went missing last week from the houses on the back roads. I have a feeling something bad happened to her.'

'Nobody young has turned up on this side. An old farmer off the back roads looking for his brother, that's all.'

'Does that mean she's alive somewhere?'

'I don't know,' he said. 'Things happen I don't know about.'

It was drizzling now. Ultra tiny raindrops. Loads of them.

'You get on home,' he said.

'Where do you go?' I said. 'I mean to sleep and all that.'

'I'm not sure what happens to me half the time. It's like I'm drunk and I just black out and then I turn up somewhere.'

'Will I see you again?'

He said he didn't know, then he asked me if I'd leave him the matches. He descended a bit and I handed them over.

I had a last drag on the cigarette and threw it on the road. A car whizzed past.

'The brakes need adjusting on that bike,' he said. 'You didn't tighten them enough when you put the pads on.'

I ignored him and started cycling.

'Be careful,' he shouted. He shouted something else too but I couldn't hear because my bike was making a funny noise with the tyre coming off the wheel and the wind had picked up and it was blowing in my face. I thought I heard him coughing his guts up when I was a bit further down the road and I thought I could feel him watching me all the way but when I turned the corner into the estate I looked back and all I saw was the black road and the rain falling out of the sky and the orange lights with one of them blinking on and off and no sign of him at all.

◆

The weather changed. I woke up and there was white swirls on the window. The world was white but it wasn't snow, it was frost. A cold snap, my mother said, and I imagined a big huge field with no grass or trees and white frost everywhere and bones sticking out of the frozen muck. I kept my hood up all the time now, even on the bus. Every sound was different. The stones and bits of glass were stuck to the road and the grass and the sheets on the line were stiff.

I got an A for an essay at school, all of it lies, nothing about what was really inside me, nothing at all. The teacher said I was a good writer. I didn't tell my mother any of this. Sometimes I didn't want her to know anything about me.

Liam Kelly brought in photos of dead babies in rubbish bins and we looked at them in religion.

Then one of the days, I told my mother a lie about going to the library and I went to the doctors in the village instead.

It was ages since I'd been to the doctor and I'd never been by myself and never to this particular doctor.

I actually found his address in the phone book.

I knew I couldn't say Down Under to a doctor so I'd decided to say that I had a rash on my penis and leave my testicles out of it altogether.

The receptionist looked at me funny and asked if I'd been there before. I said no, that we had just moved there which was sort of true even though I knew my mother would never change the old doctor from where we used to live because she'd been going there since I was born and he knew my dead father and what happened to him.

There was one other lady in the waiting room and she was in an armchair. I sat on a hard sofa. It was like being in somebody's normal house, being in the sitting room, but no telly or carpet and the curtains open so people could look right in from the street. There was a superser in the corner on low so it wasn't very warm and there was a chandelier hanging out of the ceiling with bits missing. I wondered if the receptionist was the wife or something. She gave me a form to fill out and a pen that you could click to write different colours. The blue ink part was sticking out but I clicked the green and used that instead. The form asked who my last doctor was so I just wrote that I didn't know. Then I dropped the pen and I had to look behind the sofa to get it and there was loads of dust and dead bluebottles and a dead wasp all curled up. They made me think about my father in his grave. I said please let me have a dream about my father tonight under my breath but without moving my lips. There was no spiders, dead or alive.

The one other lady in the waiting room gave me a funny smile when I sat back down. I smiled back but she looked away. Sometimes when people smile at you they're not saying I'm happy or I like you. They're saying just stay where you are and don't come near me. It was one of those. Then the receptionist came in and said to the lady that the doctor would see her and when she stood up off her chair you could see from her stomach that she was going to have a baby.

I had a baby sister who was born dead but I don't remember anything about her. My mother prayed to her even though there was no gravestone for her and she never gave her a name and even I, myself, never gave her a secret name. It is hard to name someone you never met because they were never alive even though they grew inside your mother's womb like you did. She was like a feeling more than a person. She was the same feeling for me and my mother or, at least, that's the way I saw it, a kind of a sad feeling.

But the sadness of my dead sister didn't make me sad like looking at the backs of the houses did and thinking about all the people who lived in them and went to bed in them. That was like the sadness of knowing that everybody was alive and had to put up with stuff like getting up early for school or work or having your father or your husband die on you but nobody really wanted to talk about it because they were all afraid to admit how sad and hard things could be.

No, the sadness that came with my sister who was born dead was the sadness of knowing that things could happen that could stop you living your dreams and being who you really are, and you might end up never really being able to be who you really are for various reasons.

Maybe it was all just different versions of the same sadness, and the fact that everybody was busy pretending they weren't feeling the different versions was actually the saddest thing.

The receptionist came in and took the form I'd filled out and then I read my book for a while but I couldn't really concentrate so I looked out the window. It was dark and cold and the lights on the cars were sharp and the sounds the cars made were swooshy and the windows were really clean. People walked by with hats and gloves on and scarves but no hoods. Then one hood went by but it didn't have fur around the edges. Peoples' shoes sounded pointy. Then the receptionist said the doctor would see me and I got up and went to the door where I'd seen the pregnant patient go in. I knocked and the voice said to come in, so in I went.

I was a bit afraid but the doctor had glasses and a big nose and he was about the same age as my dead father. He had a cardigan on that was brown with suede parts on the sides and he had pinstripe trousers and polished shoes and a white shirt but no tie. He didn't smile or anything but he didn't look at me funny either. There was a brown carpet and it was warm and there was cream curtains that were closed so you couldn't see out. There was a desk thing and he was sitting on one side of it. He said to sit down and I did. There was a smell of oranges and there was orange peel on a saucer on the desk on top of loads of bits of paper.

'How can I help you, young man?' said the doctor.

'I have a rash.'

'Where is this rash?' said the doctor.

'On my penis.'

I saw a film once where these children with blonde hair were out to destroy the world and they could read your mind so this man made himself think of a brick wall all the time so they couldn't read his real thoughts which were actually about killing the children. I didn't think the doctor was evil at all but I thought that he might be able to read my mind and he'd see how worried I was about the rash. I tried to think of a brick wall.

'O we'll have a quick look at that,' said the doctor. 'Why don't you come around here and take down your trousers.'

I knew that he would say that. I knew that I would have to show him my penis. I had thought about all of this so, in a way, I was ready for anything but still I felt very nervous. This was a feeling in my stomach. I stood up and went around the table. I took down my trousers to my knees, then I held up my shirt, then I pulled down my underpants. I had my eyes closed, thinking of the brick wall. I had worried that my penis would grow hard when I actually showed it to him but that definitely didn't happen. I thought of the brick wall again and again and again. I thought of all the little atoms that made up the brick wall, that in a way brick walls were soft though they looked and felt hard. I thought all of this in a few seconds, somewhere between seven and eleven seconds maybe.

'That's fine, you can pull your trousers up now.'

I opened my eyes and he was looking the other way, opening a drawer in the table, acting like what had just happened hadn't really happened and wasn't really unusual and everything was completely normal. He started to write on a piece of paper.

'I'll give you a prescription to take to the chemist. Put it on the area twice a day. Do you change your underpants every day?'

'Yes,' I said.

I liked the way he said area instead of penis and testicles. It made me feel better about everything. I buttoned my trousers and walked back to the seat at the same time. Then he handed me the piece of paper.

'This is the prescription,' he said, then he told me I had to wash the area every morning and every night before putting cream on and that I was to remember to always dry myself thoroughly after a bath.

And then it happened.

'Actually, Doctor, I have another question.'

I was back in my seat now, trousers fastened, prescription in my hand.

'What is it, son?'

'It's about my father,' I said and the words were coming out of my mouth as if I meant to say them all along even though I didn't but they kept coming out and it was definitely me who was saying them.

'He's dead,' I said. 'And, well, I was wondering, being a doctor and everything, if you could tell me, I know it sounds stupid and I'm sorry, but I was wondering if you could tell me if you've ever seen a soul leaving a body when a person dies.'

I imagined putting my hand inside the brick wall like I could cut through stone and cement, down into the atoms, where everything was just the same mush, my hand and the wall, and everything melted together and was the same.

'That's a big question to be asking a doctor,' he said.

He was smiling but it was definitely a smile that said I like you so that sort of encouraged me.

'You see, I'm trying to find out if there is life after death because I miss my father and I have dreams about him and the other day I saw a ghost though not my father's ghost although the dreams I have of my father are real enough as if he is alive in another dimension or something. I don't know where this dimension is or if I'm just dreaming it.'

I moved my hand through the brick wall and it sort of parted like the Red Sea for Moses but, in a way, the wall and my hand joined together too because everything is basically the same and I started to turn into mush starting with my hand and moving up my arm.

The doctor took an orange out of one of the drawers and started peeling it. A little drop of orange juice squirted out of the orange and shot across the table and landed somewhere behind my chair.

'No,' he said, 'I have never seen anything like a soul leaving a body,' and he was very, very serious here, 'but I have felt something in the room when I've been with people who are dying, and I've seen my fair share of dying, and I've always felt that the something I felt was God, and I mean God in a way that's a million times more complicated and a million times simpler than what you hear about at school from your teachers or at mass when the priest talks about God.'

'I don't know what you mean,' I said.

The smell of orange got stronger and stronger. I stopped turning into mush.

'I'm not sure what I mean myself,' he said, 'except that when you die I believe something happens rather than nothing happens.'

'I still don't know what you mean,' I said.

He put a big piece of orange in his mouth and made a funny face and chewed for a while and then he said:

'I mean I think your father is probably in heaven, wherever that is, and he is looking after you in ways that maybe you and I don't understand.'

I said nothing. I could feel my eyes watering and I didn't want him to see it. I thought about the atoms in the brick wall and the atoms in my hand and how my father's atoms were mostly lying on the bottom of his coffin now, and every second extra bits of him crumbled off and dissolved into atoms, and then I thought about what the teacher said about bricks running down the road and jumping on top of one another to build the school because that's what you might as well believe if you didn't believe in God. I thought about all of these things at the same time and separately and the smell of oranges was everywhere and I thought my dead father will never get this smell again and my dead sister never smelled it in the first place so I breathed it in and all the orangey atoms went into my lungs and into my bloodstream and I realised I was really hungry and I looked over the table at the doctor who was chewing his orange and I said:

'I don't think I believe in God.'

The doctor was looking at me but he didn't look annoyed and, after approximately seven seconds, he said: 'Maybe you don't have to believe in God, maybe your father is doing the believing in God for you.'

I thought about this for approximately five seconds and I decided it didn't make any sense.

'Are you saying that my dead father knows there is a God so I don't have to worry about whether there is or not?' I wanted to be sure that I'd heard him properly.

The doctor made his head go up and down. He was smiling.

And suddenly the whole world was just really sad, and I could see that the doctor was as confused as I was, and when I saw this, a tear actually came out of my eye and rolled down my cheek. And then another one came, and this one rolled down and fell off, and I was staring at the doctor, feeling sorry for the pair of us really, but he was looking a bit pleased with himself so I didn't have the heart to tell him that I thought what he'd just said was stupid, and then I could feel my face starting to go out of control like a monster was taking me over and forcing me to smile a big huge smile that I really didn't want to smile.

It actually hurt the muscles in my cheeks and I think I started making crying noises a bit like the hiccups, and I looked down at my lap and I saw a tear fall onto my trousers and make a stain and then another one and another one and another one.

'I'm sorry, doctor,' I said, 'I'm sorry,' and I think I said it a few more times but my voice sounded like a girl crying, and the doctor came over to me and knelt in front of me and his voice was really quiet and really deep and he said not to be worrying, but I wasn't worrying, I wasn't even sorry, I was just thinking about my father and how he was dead as a doornail and all the dreaming about him couldn't make him come back, and even if he was looking after me from heaven, which I didn't actually believe he was, how that just wasn't the same as being alive, and I wanted him to be alive and everything to be normal again, and him to be saying do you want to go for a walk, pal? and us to be going for the walk, and then maybe us to be in the pub and him to be having a pint of Guinness and me to be having a coke and a packet of cheese and onion, and then us to be home and him to be asleep in his chair by the fire, and me to be watching the wrestling on the telly, and it to be raining outside.

Anyway, when I eventually stopped crying the doctor went out to the receptionist and I could hear him asking her to get a glass of lemonade but what she actually brought in was a glass of American Cream Soda with ice cubes in it which was one of my favourites. It had a straw in it and patterns of daisies on the glass.

I kept saying I was sorry but the doctor told me to stop saying it so I did. Then he said he was sorry to hear about my father and he asked me how my mother was and I said she was ok. I asked him if he knew my mother and he said no and he laughed and said I was to come and see him any time I needed to but he needed to see other people now and could I finish my American Cream Soda in the waiting room.

He was being kind but I didn't want to go back in the waiting room so I drank it all down there and then and said thank you.

The receptionist wasn't there when I went out and I was glad of that.

As I said previously, the street was all dark and cold and the lights were really bright and the cars made swooshing sounds and peoples' shoes sounded pointy. I stopped for a second and looked into the doctor's waiting room from the street and there were two people sitting in there, a man and a woman, sitting beside each other, but you couldn't tell if they were husband and wife or even if they were friends but they were sitting on the sofa that I had sat on, the one with the dead bluebottles underneath and the dust and the one dead wasp and no spiders to be seen, and they looked lost and sad even though they were right beside each other and probably touching each other's legs because it was a small sofa and it would be hard to sit on without touching the person beside you.

Anyway, after me doing a lot of worrying about it, the lady in the chemist gave me the ointment without even looking like she knew what area it was for so that was a relief and by the time I got home I was beginning to feel a bit better about everything.

The fire was really hot and my mother was sitting watching the telly and I could tell she was in a good mood for some reason. I needed to keep her in a good mood for the meeting at the school later that week so I stayed around and chatted and told her the dinner she had kept warm on top of a pot of water on the cooker was lovely even though I threw out the pork chop when she wasn't looking.

After I'd eaten I made us a cup of tea and we sat down and watched stuff on the telly. And then I did tell her about getting the A for the essay and she was delighted. To be honest, it was easy being nice to my mother when we were getting on and she was in a good mood and I was in a good mood. And that was often enough in the end because basically we sort of liked each other and that was that.

◆

The week went on like that with my mother and me in good moods and watching telly on the freezing nights. I spoke to Angela on the phone a few times. She said she was writing a big poem about how sad she was about Marion. She didn't mention the novel we were writing and I thought that maybe she was bored with the story of the girls who travelled back in time. I had kind of decided that I wanted to write something different too but I wasn't sure what it was. I just knew it was going to be about stuff people didn't normally want to know about.

Not much else really happened. My mother went to the

meeting at the school but she was fine about everything when she came back and she said the teachers thought I was doing ok again so there was nothing to worry about though they said I needed to pay attention every day and not just sometimes and to stop daydreaming and get my homework done and that I had a great imagination.

Then on the Saturday, my mother wasn't working so she asked me to come with her to the food co-op at Clonduff House to do some work there. She said she'd give me extra pocket money so I went even though I didn't really want to. The thing was I didn't want to do the work (moving things around so they could paint the room where they stored the stuff they sold in the shop) but I did want to see inside Clonduff House properly and money was always a good thing.

I was hoping it would only be the two of us but then she said Mr Daly would be coming too and I was always nervous when it had anything to do with neighbours and them asking me what team I followed or if I had a girlfriend or something. My mother never seemed to notice how horrible this was for me or maybe she pretended she didn't.

Anyway, there was nobody else there when we got there and I could tell my mother was sort of excited to have keys and be able to get in with nobody else around.

Clonduff House wasn't a giant mansion or anything. It

was only three stories high although it had a basement too. First there was this patio kind of thing with glass windows everywhere and a glass door and then the actual front door. Once you were inside it had three big rooms on the ground floor (where they had the disco and the shop) and four or five empty ones on the floor above that. Everywhere was dusty. There was a toilet on each floor but none of them smelled very clean. You couldn't actually get up to the very top floor because the stairs just weren't there. There was just a hole in the ceiling where the staircase should go and you could see where it had been attached to the wall but there was no sign of the actual staircase anywhere. What could happen in a house to make a whole staircase disappear?

There was a bockedy stairs that went down into the basement and there was no furniture anywhere and the place needed a paint and the windows were dirty and the curtains were filthy. You could feel the dust in the air when you breathed in.

Our job was to move the boxes of washing powder and shampoo and tins of beans and peas and biscuits (they were like cheaper versions of the proper ones that we had at home) from one room in the basement into the other so Mr Daly could come around later and paint it.

My mother was always interested if things were going to be painted or carpets were going to be put down or curtains put up.

There was a kettle and mugs and a radio in the shop room so we had a cup of tea before we set to work. She turned on the superser and opened a packet of biscuits from the shop.

'These biscuits are rubbish,' she said, but she kept eating them and so did I. She looked sort of young in the light from the morning coming through the windows and I liked that. Some days she looked kind of glamorous and then other days she didn't at all. This was a glamorous day. It had nothing to do with the weather or the time of the year. For example, she'd looked really tired all the time during the summer when we'd first moved to Clonduff.

'O, I've been meaning to tell you,' she said, dunking a biscuit, 'I've started reading that book, Wuthering Heights.'

I pretended not to hear.

'That girl you like wrote the song about it,' she kept going, 'the one who screams like a banshee.'

She put the whole biscuit into her mouth.

I knew what she was talking about alright because we'd had a row about it when the song came out and as part of my argument to get her to actually like Kate Bush I'd told her it was based on a book that I would have to do for school.

'Mr Daly lent it to me,' she said.

'She doesn't scream like a banshee,' I said.

She made her eyes go up and around which meant she was beginning to be in a bad mood and so we finished our tea without saying anything else, both of us sort of sulking. Then she just said come on and we got to work carrying the boxes from one room into the other. I think we were glad that we hadn't had a proper argument and lifting the boxes and moving them needed us to work together and that sort of made everything feel better. I'm not sure why.

Most of what we were carrying was washing powder, then biscuits, then shampoo. We had a kind of old trolley thing that squeaked when you moved it. Some of the boxes had blood dripping out of them. They were the ones with the nuns' and priests' head inside in them. My mother didn't seem to notice this so I said nothing. It was hard work but I could tell she wanted us to finish it so I kept going with her until it was all moved.

It took ages but eventually we got everything moved.

'What happens now?' I said.

She said something about Mr Daly coming and us having to wait around and let him in but I wasn't interested so I said I wanted to go and we were about to have another argument when all of a sudden someone banged at the front door and we went quiet.

'You go.'

'No, you go.'

Then we both said we'd go at exactly the same time. The banging came again.

We headed up the stairs together, laughing and pushing each other to get there first.

'Maybe it's the ghost,' she said.

'What ghost?'

'The lady who haunts the house. They found her in the pond. Strangled.'

We were at the door now.

'Ask Mr Daly,' she said.

She opened the door and there he was. I had met him once before but I hadn't had a good look at him or paid any attention. This time I did. He was skinny and grey like he had no blood in him at all and the big smile he had on his face when he saw my mother went away as soon as he saw me.

'Hello Mr Daly,' said my mother. 'I was just telling John about the ghost and he doesn't believe me.'

'I never said I didn't believe you.'

'O it's true, alright,' said Mr Daly. 'She was the lady of the house. I'm trying to lay my hands on some photographs of her.'

And in he came.

'I'm actually going now,' I said. I didn't like him being

here even if he did know about the ghost.

'Where are you off to in such a hurry?'

'Nowhere.'

'Well say hello to Mr Daly first.'

I said hello and he said hello back.

I got my anorak from the basement and when I came back up they were just standing there looking at me. I could tell they'd been talking about me.

'I'll drop around with those old photographs to show you sometime,' he said.

'Ok,' I said, backing down the hallway towards the front door.

My mother shouted goodbye as I left and then the door slammed behind me as if I had done it on purpose because I was in a mood.

I stood in the glass patio bit for a while just looking at the park and the sky. Everything was still and you couldn't hear any noise from inside in the house either. The sky was quiet and the clouds were quiet and the trees were all lined up around the park. Most of them had no leaves and all their branches and twigs were pointing in different directions. The grass was mainly green with brown patches of muck around the goalposts. It was like I was in a 3D picture of Clonduff Park with the house in the middle of it and me in the glass patio bit at the front of the house. Then when I moved my head down so that

I was looking at the ground under my feet I could see the fur around my hood and then a patch of broken concrete floor that was the colour of liver and kidneys before you fry them.

I saw this postcard once that had a funny drawing of this man at the seaside and when he was putting his swimming togs on he looked down and he could only see his belly because he was so fat. He never saw his penis or testicles again. He was sad but you were supposed to laugh at him.

I didn't laugh.

Even my fingers were fat.

I imagined my fingers closing around Mr Daly's throat as he begged me to spare his life. Only if you leave my mother alone! For she will never marry the likes of you!

I'd scream the last bit, pressing his Adam's Apple into the back of his throat as his eyes popped out of his head on stalks.

This vision of Mr Daly made me feel weird so I went out of the glass patio bit and started walking across the park. I didn't really know where to go. What if my mother did fall in love with him? I would never know where to go again. I would have to move out and live in the caravan on the pig farm. The superser would run out of gas and I'd freeze to death and that would serve everybody right. They would find me all frozen and white in the caravan.

A cold snap got him, my mother would say. But she would not be Madame X at my funeral. She would be just plain old Mrs Daly and my father and me would haunt her dreams for eternity.

In the middle of the park I stopped walking. There was nobody else around. Usually there'd be boys playing football so I wouldn't walk into the middle. I turned around in a circle and saw the trees and the grass and the sky and the goal posts and Clonduff House and the side of the estate and again it was like I was at the centre of everything and there was nobody else like me except maybe Angela but even she was different in the end. Everybody and everything was separate from everybody and everything else.

There was four crows standing around. I tried to imagine being them and having friends who looked exactly like you and you hated everybody different to you.

That was probably a better life than being in a field just being me, different from everybody else.

I ran at the crows shouting fuck off and off they fucked, all of them together in the same direction, laughing at me and going *kwarrrkk*, and the sound of their *kwarrrkk* seemed as much part of the morning and the park as the sky and the trees and the grass.

So maybe everything was connected if you were a

crow.

Then I stood for a little while more in the park and I sang the Kate Bush song really loud and then I headed for home.

Angela and me hadn't really spoken to each other that week and I was actually a bit worried that she'd gone off me, so I phoned her when I got in. She came on the phone and I knew right away everything was fine. She told me stuff that girls at school were saying things about her sister, that she was a slut and everything, and how her mother had to go into the school and give out, and how her mother was crying every night, and her father was out drinking all the time, and him and the mother weren't talking. She didn't seem sad, and she said she was writing loads of poetry.

We didn't talk about the novel. It definitely looked like both of us were sick of it. And I didn't tell her anything about going to see Tony and the ghost of FlanaganBrannigan or going to the doctor and getting the prescription either.

I did tell her about Mr Daly and she said he sounded like a slithering snake.

Then we arranged for me to cycle up to her house the next day and then we said goodbye.

I got off the phone and went upstairs to do my exercises with the Gloria Gaynor on. After that I read my book in the bath until the water went nearly cold. My mother came home when I was still in the bath and I could tell she was in a good mood by her voice when she called to see if I was in.

I dried myself, spending extra time on the area, then I got the cream out of the wardrobe and applied it, and then I got dressed and went downstairs. My mother had the fire lit and we had a cup of tea and read our books as it got dark outside only talking now and again but nothing important.

The film that night was a cowboy so we weren't interested and we just read our books. My mother actually held her book (i.e. Wuthering Heights) up in the air at one point and said that it was getting better at last, that it had taken a while for the story to get started.

I said I thought books should be exciting from the first page, and she said she gave them until the second chapter but that Wuthering Heights had definitely taken a lot longer.

Anyway, that night I had the dream with my father in it. He came into my room on his floating throne and stopped beside my bed. He had a crown on except it was like this pin cushion crown thing in the china cabinet downstairs that had a measuring tape inside in it. He was all dressed up like he was going to a dinner dance with my mother and he had the cage in his stomach again but this time it was empty. He said the baby version of me had disappeared and he didn't know where I (i.e. the baby me) was gone.

He was roaring and crying and his clothes were all wringing wet from the tears and the crown was sideways on his head and the tears were causing problems in the engine of the floating throne. Orange sparks were coming flying out of it and landing on the carpet. I told him not to worry, that I was fine, but inside I felt that something wasn't right.

When I woke up from the dream, I could hear wolves howling in Clonduff Park and the big purple moon outside my window had actual craters on it.

❖

Next morning was Sunday. In the paper Dear Valerie said queers weren't normal people and that's why they had sex in toilets.

Liam Kelly said queers just stuck it up each other's arses. That sounded sore.

We had roast beef for dinner, and Cidona with ice cubes, and my mother and me touched our glasses off each other and had a big mouthful before we even started eating.

'He'd be having his Guinness if he was here,' she said,

and I thought about telling her about the dreams I was having about him, and about how me as a baby had gone missing from the cage inside in his stomach, and he was roaring and crying and his floating throne was breaking down. But I decided not to. I couldn't tell her about FlanaganBrannigan or the rash down under or Tony in the workman's hut either. All these things were secrets I suppose but not just because I liked not telling her, it was also because I didn't think she would like to know.

The dinner was actually lovely even though I threw most of it out when she wasn't looking. Afterwards I did the washing up and she sat down with the paper. Then I got my bike out and fixed the puncture. My uncle Brian had brought new tyres around and I put them on and then I adjusted the brakes and off I went.

I was going out the gate when my mother called out the window to ask me if I'd be back for tea and I said I didn't know, that I was going up to Angela's. She made an *ooooh* sound as if Angela was my girlfriend. Sometimes she seemed to enjoy annoying me. It was one of the reasons why I hated her knowing any of my stuff.

It was cold and the sky was blue and I had my hood up. Clonduff was quiet enough on Sunday afternoons. I saw no boys playing football or hanging around throwing stones and there was no cars on the road. I was a bit depressed even though I was on my bike. I suppose I was worried that I was a queer and I wasn't normal.

Everything was quiet except for the sound of my wheels going around and bird noises coming from all directions and the odd car whizzing past.

It wasn't long before I could smell the pig shed.

I stopped and leaned the bike against the gate, pulled down my hood and lit a cigarette. It lit the first time and I sat on the gate smoking in the quiet. There was no wind and I practised smoke rings but none of them worked. A robin hopped out of a bush and landed on a twig. The cigarette tasted extra smoky. There was no sign of any people anywhere and no *oink* sounds were coming out of the pig shed although there was a horrible smell even worse than normal even though the smoke covered it up a bit.

Little flies were flying around.

I started singing the Gloria Gaynor to cheer myself up and there I was smoking and singing away when out of nowhere I noticed a funny voice was singing along with me. It was really weird and at first I wondered if I was going mad and imagining it all so I stopped singing and when I did the voice stopped too.

I had a drag on the cigarette and looked around but there was nobody to be seen and the only sound was a bit of wind blowing through the bushes and trees so after approximately ten seconds I started singing again.

The voice started again!

I stopped.

It stopped.

I sat on the gate listening.

Nothing.

The sky was blue with an airplane really high and all the little branches and twigs and leaves moving around in circles. I was beginning to feel like something terrible was going to happen. This was a feeling in my stomach and so for approximately fifteen seconds I didn't move or make noise except to smoke and during that time it was as if I wasn't actually there but nobody else was either and so I began to sing again, really low.

Smoke was coming out with the words.

The voice started singing again too!

I stopped but this time the voice just went on:

Go on now, Go! Walk out that door! Don't turn around now! Cause you're not welcome anymore...

It knew all the words!!!

I had the last drag and threw the butt in the grass.

'Who's there?' I shouted.

The singing stopped but no answer came.

Slowly, slowly, I got down off the gate.

I meant to get straight on the bike and cycle off but then I realised I was on the pig shed side anyway. The bike was on the other side so I'd have to get back over the gate. The weird voice was on this side.

Where I was.

I stood very still and listened but there was nothing.

The whole world was quiet. Even the flies were all landed.

The shed was long with the opening at the other end away from me. You could see it through the hedge from the road but I'd never actually looked inside.

I started to walk up the side of the shed.

There was nettles everywhere.

My heart was beating fast and I could actually hear my clothes moving and the grass and nettles bending under my feet and being pushed out of the way by my shoes and legs.

After approximately forty seconds (I stopped a couple of times on the way to listen but I could hear nothing) I eventually got to the end of the shed. The smell was rotten. I peeped around the corner. There was nobody there. I looked up the field and there was nobody there. The pink caravan and the old cottage were there but no sign of anybody.

A black crow landed on a branch that was sticking out of the hedge.

'You're mad and you imagined everything,' he said. His beady eye glinted and he flew off over the hedge to another field somewhere. He didn't fly very high, more like a big hop.

Everything still and quiet.

I stuck my head around to have a look inside in the shed. It was long and dark and little shafts of light like ultra tiny sunbeams shone down through the joins in the sheets of tin that made up the roof and walls. You couldn't see the ground properly. It could have been a huge black hole but really it was just an empty old pig shed. I was wondering where the pigs had all gone when the voice came and actually told me:

'The pigs are all after being taken away down the country to be killed.'

It came out of the black darkness, somewhere in the shed, the middle of nowhere really, waiting, waiting for me.

The funny thing was that I wasn't scared, and even though the voice sounded like it was from a horror film, and even though the shed was dark, and even though everything should have been really scary, it just wasn't, and that was because whatever was in the shed wanted me to be alright.

'Who are you?' I said.

'I am RottingDead,' she said. I knew she was a she. I knew that she was in pain in the way a he wouldn't be. Or the majority of hes anyway. I knew this but I didn't know why I knew it or what it really meant.

'Was that you singing a minute ago?' I said.

'That was me singing.'

'Where are you?' I said. 'I can't see.'

'I'm here. Right in the middle.'

And then I could sort of make out a shape. Or at least I thought I could. And maybe an eye and a bit of hair and a pointy-up ear. Sort of floating.

'What happened to you?' I said.

'A boy killed me and cut my head off.'

'Are you the horse that got killed in the field and got your head cut off?'

'I am the head of that horse. But I don't know where the rest of me is. I'm stuck on a pole.'

'I know who did this,' I said.

'I don't like being like this,' she said. 'Do you know where the rest of me is?'

She began to cry.

Everything seemed so awful and sad.

'Don't cry,' I said, even though I was starting to cry myself. Tears were actually coming out of my eyes and rolling down my cheeks.

I climbed over the wooden fence that blocked the way. It was darker inside and my feet were sinking into the muck and the smell. I could see the shape of RottingDead in front of me down in the dark. She was the episode of Star Trek with the screaming skulls. She was one of the skulls. She was the banshee crying for my father in the grave and, at the same time, she was exactly like my father in the grave with the bits of skin peeling off around the eyes and the nose and the mouth and the bone showing with the bits of hair and the teeth on the outside.

Her atoms were everywhere and she was returning to mush and crying.

I tripped and fell down and there was something else down there, down in the mush, sucking me down all around me, all cold and rotten.

The world of mush and RottingDead.

And I heard RottingDead say 'I miss you, John, I wish you…' and I was crawling down to her, down into the darkness, dissolving into mush and crying, and the ground was bumpy and soft at the same time, and the whole world was a long tunnel, black with stars shrunk down to atoms, and my head was exploding with polka dots and pinstripes, and there was nothing, nothing at all, just the long tunnel, and the mush and the dark and RottingDead for ever and ever…

The Tale of RottingDead
and FlanaganBrannigan

On a housing estate called ClonduffSiberia deep in the middle of nowhere really, the body of a horse named RottingDead lies buried in the garden of a house that no family has moved into yet.

The body of this horse does not have the head attached but it does have a heart, and its heart is lonely and filled with longing.

Now the garden where this horse is buried is just down from another garden where a lad called Tony lives in a hut. Tony used to live in the caravan by the pig shed on the back roads but Mickey and Pat, the farmers, went and died and so he had to move.

Not many people actually know that the body of RottingDead is buried here but there is a ghost called FlanaganBrannigan who knows exactly where the body is because he was there, floating and hovering, when RottingDead was killed and he also knows that the boy who did the killing goes by the name of Paul the Rapist.

You see, FlanaganBrannigan can read peoples' minds and see through walls. He knows what you're thinking and what you're doing. Even when you're thinking and doing things you don't want anyone to know about, not even yourself sometimes.

And that's how he knows that Paul the Rapist is the one who shot RottingDead with the crossbow, who gouged out one of her eyes, who chopped off her head with a saw and stuck it in a Roches Stores bag with a picture of Santy Claus and his reindeers and his sleigh flying across the sky and over the rooftops with snow piled up everywhere, even on the actual letters that spell Roches Stores.

He knows that Paul the Rapist used a JCB to bury the body and he knows that Paul the Rapist then legged it up the back roads with a bottle of cider in one hand and the other hand holding the bag with the head in it and dripping and dribbling a trail of little red plops.

You see, Paul the Rapist had a plan to put the head of RottingDead into Tony's bed in the caravan to get at him because he'd stolen Marion away.

(This was before Tony moved out of the caravan and down into the hut in the garden of the new houses that weren't finished).

(Marion was always flying around on her bike and all the boys wanted to go out with her).

Well, that was the plan anyway and Flanagan-Brannigan knew about the plan but unfortunately he never found out what happened next in the plan because he's actually kind of trapped around ClonduffSiberia i.e. if he wanders off too far from the roads around the estate he sort of disappears or goes unconscious or stops being alive (if you could ever actually describe a ghost as being alive, that is).

It looks like FlanaganBrannigan is stuck in ClonduffSiberia because the fat boy lives there and it looks like the only time he can actually leave is when the fat boy leaves too. In fact, FlanaganBrannigan seems to have some connection to the fat boy, he just isn't sure what it is. But when the fat boy goes anywhere, FlanaganBrannigan can go as well.

(The fat boy doesn't usually go far though. The library or school mostly).

Anyway this day the fat boy goes up to the pig shed on the back roads and FlanaganBrannigan goes too and while the fat boy is unconscious with his face down in the muck and the mush, doesn't FlanaganBrannigan get into a conversation with RottingDead's head which is stuck on a pole, and doesn't he commiserate with her on her lack of a body, and doesn't he tell her not to be worrying because he actually knows where the rest of her is buried.

Well RottingDead, as you can imagine, is absolutely delighted to hear this and, with FlanaganBrannigan's help, she slides herself off the pole and the pair of them float and hover and fly back to the estate to find her body for her (but not before FlanaganBrannigan stops to check that the fat boy is still breathing and not actually dead or anything).

So, off they go, the head of RottingDead and FlanaganBrannigan with his dirty grey mac flipping and flapping and floating and hovering in the sky over the fields and houses full of families, down to the garden where the body of RottingDead is buried at the back of the houses that aren't finished yet.

And sure enough, as soon as they get there doesn't the head of RottingDead start singing and whinnying the Gloria Gaynor song, and under the ground the heart of RottingDead hears this singing and whinnying and recognises her own voice and is absolutely delighted because music and singing is the language of the heart. And that's how the body of RottingDead comes back to life and starts stretching and moving under the ground and making a big effort and then a huge, big effort and then a huge, big, massive effort and eventually the body of RottingDead manages to push right through the weight of the muck and the mush and up she goes out of the ground, and the garden shakes and moves a bit like a tiny earthquake of approximately two point five on the Richter Scale, and a big bump grows and the bump splits open and the headless corpse of RottingDead actually comes out of the ground and gives herself a good shake to get all the muck and dirt off.

Meanwhile, down in the hut three gardens away, Tony is thinking about kissing Marion and about how much he misses her and he's doing something he doesn't want anybody else to see or know about and he's doing it with his own spit and not with Deep Heat ointment, and FlanaganBrannigan can actually see this through the wall but he doesn't mind and he says nothing and the result of Tony being busy thinking about Marion is that even though he sort of hears all the singing and commotion that's going on outside he just ignores it, and that's how he misses the very unusual spectacle of RottingDead's headless body rising from the grave, and how he misses RottingDead's head actually descending out of the sky and joining onto her body, and her hardly able to believe that she is one whole horse again even though she is rotting and stinks of death and there's a kind of a seam around her neck where it joins, and when she goes up on her back legs and makes her front legs go around because she's so delighted doesn't her head slide off and fall onto the ground and it has to float back up and reattach itself.

Even still she's extremely grateful to Flanagan-Brannigan for reuniting her and she allows him to ride on her back in the sky and clouds over Clonduff-Siberia, and it's lashing livers and kidneys and blood and guts and she's whinnying the Gloria Gaynor song and just then, at that very moment, all the millions and millions of sperm get ejaculated out of Tony's penis and testicles and he makes funny faces and shows his teeth and there's bits of food stuck in them in the grooves where the teeth join the gums and there's punk music on the transistor and Tony says the name of his one true love over and over and over like it's a magic spell that will make everything better again - Marion Marion Marion Marion *- and even when he's finished saying it his lips keep moving because he's saying it under his breath and then magic actually happens and the transistor changes stations and Gloria Gaynor comes on singing her song at the same time as RottingDead is singing it and all the nuns' and priests' heads in all the cardboard boxes in Clonduff House join in with the singing and all these old ladies in the nude are dancing with devils with vampire teeth and forked tongues and tails and feet like old goats and all the wolves are howling to the music and the bats of Clonduff park are singing along but you can't hear them because their voices are outside human hearing so you can only see their lips move, and Tony is keeping his eyes squeezed closed but tears are coming out anyway and one silver tear rolls sideways from his left eye to his left ear and one silver tear rolls sideways from his right eye to his right ear and then he falls asleep for a little while and all the singing comes to an end and all the nuns' and priests' heads shut up again and all the cardboard boxes go quiet so you'd never be able to tell what's* *actually inside in them and all the dancing stops and the wolves and bats stop singing too and it stops raining blood and guts and RottingDead is delighted with herself, riding off into the purple sunset with FlanaganBrannigan on her back and his grey mac flipping and flapping, and even though frightening things have happened, they've now stopped happening, and everything is absolutely ok again.*

(Except for Paul the Rapist because he was the one who caused all this trouble in the first place and so Rottingdead and FlanaganBrannigan go and scare the shite out of him by turning up in his bedroom when he's putting on his pyjamas and getting ready for bed and RottingDead makes her head come off and fly around the room with blood spurting out of her neck and her whinnying in a blood curdling fashion and FlanaganBrannigan makes the skin peel off his face until his eyeballs are hanging out of his head on stalks and his teeth are like vampire's teeth stuck in a screaming skull and the smell is the horrible stench of death and Paul the Rapist actually shites himself in his pyjama bottoms because he's so frightened and he's screaming and crying and it's all running down his legs and on the bedsheets and doesn't his father

come upstairs and beat the rest of the shite out of him for being a coward and doing a shite all over the bedroom and being just a stupid boy and not actually a man like he's been brought up to be).

And, anyway, that's actually the only bad thing that happened that night and, me, I'm the fat boy with his face in the mush who lived to tell the tale so, you see, I didn't die in the pig shed, no sirree, because my best friend came to rescue me. And my best friend is called Angela and my name is John and I actually wrote this.

'John! Wake up! It's me!'

It was dark around the edges and buzzing in my ears.

'Where am I?'

'You're in the pig shed,' said Angela's voice.

I could sort of see her face.

I tried to move but I actually felt weak.

'Is RottingDead here?' I lifted my head to look.

The pole was there alright, stuck in the ground, but RottingDead's head was gone.

'What are you talking about?'

'There was a horse's head,' I said. 'It was weird...' I stopped talking then, mainly because I wasn't sure I could explain properly what had happened.

'This place stinks,' said Angela. She gave me her hand so I could stand up.

It was the first time we'd held hands in ages. I was a bit dizzy. Her hand was lovely and warm. She held me as we walked out of the dark and into the daylight. She helped me climb over the fence at the end and then we were in the field and it was bright. It was the girl doing it for the boy. Rain was drizzling down and the grass and bushes and nettles etc. were all shiny or extra green or something. I could still smell the bad smell but the air was better outside the shed. I took a deep breath in and then let it out.

'How did you find me?'

'I was coming to meet you and I saw your bike locked to the gate.'

'You're my saviour,' I said.

I reached into my pocket and got out my last two cigarettes. They were a little bit crumpled. I put both of them in my mouth and lit them. They lit first time. I gave Angela hers and we sat down on a tree that was lying on its side. Her hair was all stuck to her head from the ultra tiny raindrops and I wanted to tell her that I loved her and we were going to be friends forever and ever but I didn't. I blew a perfect smoke ring instead. My first one ever. It was like a space station made of smoke and you could see it rolling around itself as it got bigger and moved away from my lips.

'That's a good one,' she said.

I looked at her, feeling proud of myself, and we both started breaking our hearts for some reason, and the little movements we made, and maybe the breeze coming out of our mouths and noses, made the spaceship crumble in the air and all the little astronauts got sucked out into space and died and the whole thing disappeared into nothing.

Then we just sat there, getting wet from the rain and talking about stuff that had nothing to do with me and the pig shed. Angela had the David Bowie tape she'd made me with her and she did an impression of David Bowie doing the poem about the future when everybody lives in skyscrapers and Diamond Dogs rule the world.

When she was finished she said let's get on the bikes and go up to her house. I had muck all over my clothes but she said her mother and father were out and we could smoke and listen to music really loud.

It sounded like a good idea and so off we went on our bikes.

The squashed dog or fox was still on the road down from Angela's house but it was flatter than before. I cycled right over it.

We left the bikes in front of the house. Angela said nobody ever robbed anything around there.

The downstairs bit of the house was really big with big windows looking out onto the front garden and then onto the road. It was definitely as if the view was there for you to just sit on the sofa and spend time looking at it.

The front garden had a lawn with no weeds and two deck chairs and a little table and rose bushes and a wall and then the road with the squashed dog or fox. On the other side of the road there was a hedge and then a small hill behind that with no houses on it. The telly wasn't turned on so you could hear birds singing outside. You could see poles with telephone wires and crows sitting on them. The view from the front of my house was just more houses, exactly the same, and poles for the lights and telephones and baby trees with metal cage things around them, and even most of them had no trees in them because boys had killed them. The view from the back of my house was the depressing gardens with walls around them and all of them exactly the same (although some of them were painted different colours) and there was clothes lines and rubbish like old motor bikes and broken cars and fridges in most of the gardens.

I asked Angela what the view was at the back of her house and she brought me into the kitchen and you could see a big, huge field out the window.

'Magic mushrooms grow in that field,' she said. 'They

give you special visions.'

I'd had enough of visions for that day so I didn't say anything.

Timmy followed us into the kitchen, walking really slowly with his tail between his legs like he was really sad. Hair was starting to grow back on the part of him where he had his operation but he still looked miserable.

Angela made a fuss of him and told him he was lovely and then I petted him and bent down and kissed him and scratched his ears and his tail came up a little bit and gave a couple of wags.

Angela whispered to me that he missed Marion and he gave a whimper when he heard her name.

Then we took toast and glasses of orange upstairs to Angela's bedroom and sat on the floor and listened to the David Bowie record (which I was beginning to like). Timmy came with us and lay on the bed licking his penis and testicles. The duvet cover was white with a pale blue pinstripe and you could see a patch where Timmy had been asleep and left his hairs, a mixture of colours, stuck on the cover.

When the record was finished we were just lying there looking at the ceiling, smoking a cigarette, and Angela asked me about what happened in the pigshed.

The smoke was getting sucked up and out the window really fast.

'I don't really know what happened,' I said.

She asked me if I remembered anything at all and I just said I heard something so I went in to investigate.

'What did you hear?'

'I heard a funny voice, I think. The shed was dark. I must have hit my head.'

She asked me what the funny voice said and I just said I couldn't remember. Then she gave me the cigarette to smoke and went and put on the Kate Bush song really loud which was good because I didn't really want to keep talking about the shed and anyway Angela was doing the Kate Bush dance now, making her arms go up and down and around and singing the song with her eyes closed. Timmy stuck his nose up in the air and opened his mouth a bit and a long whine came out.

The thing was I did actually remember what happened in the shed. I remembered seeing RottingDead's head on a pole, and her being sad and crying and everything, and I remembered falling down into the muck and seeing stars like in cartoons and everything going dark but I didn't want to tell anybody about all of that.

I didn't want to tell anybody about crawling in the muck down to RottingDead and everything turning to mush.

I didn't think Angela would think I was mad if I told her but I did think she might laugh or just turn it into a ghost adventure story or something. It was more than that and that's why I wanted to keep it to myself.

When the song was over Angela stopped her dancing and jumped onto the bed to kiss Timmy. His tail wagged and his tongue went into her mouth. She moved her head away but she didn't say *ugh*.

Then, when she was finished rolling around in the bed with Timmy, she turned to me: 'Let's go into Marion's room. I want to show you something.'

Her hair was sticking up everywhere. I threw the cigarette butt out the window and followed her out of the room.

Marion's bedroom was the next door on the landing. Timmy stayed behind on the bed even though I called him. Angela said he hadn't gone into the bedroom since Marion disappeared.

She opened the door only a bit and stuck her head in as if she was half expecting somebody to be in there. Then when she'd had a look at the room for herself she pushed the door open for me to come in behind her.

It was actually very exciting to be in Marion's room. I'd never met her so this was the next best thing and, in a way, her bedroom was like a lot of clues that she left behind.

The room was the same size and shape as Angela's but everything else about it was different. Where Angela's room was tidy and clean, Marion's was sort of messy. The sideways ceiling had posters stuck all over it so you could hardly see any of the wallpaper and some of the posters were actually falling off at the edges. The light hanging out of the ceiling was a big paper ball, like the moon, and the posters were pop stars I didn't know. A lot of them were punk rockers. One was just a sad looking soldier, then just the universe with all the stars and planets, and then a man with really long hair lying down in a dress. It said The Man Who Sold The World.

'That's David Bowie,' said Angela. 'He wears dresses too.'

The wall paper, what you could see of it under all the posters, was actually chipboard painted pink and there was an ashtray on the table beside the bed and a lamp that had a sparkly red scarf thrown over it. The bed had a purple duvet and there was a dressing table, a bit like my mother's except it was white (my mother's was brown) and it had loads of stuff on it like golden boxes and perfume bottles and a silver hand with rings on it and a little glass swan with bracelets and necklaces thrown over it. There was talcum powder on the carpet and you could see footprints in it. There was furry slippers and high heels and sandals on the floor and the door of the wardrobe was open because it was jam packed with so many skirts and blouses. There was a doll on top of the wardrobe in a box that said I TALK I WALK I CRAWL and a record player but I didn't see any records I knew. Some of the records were out of their sleeves and just balanced against the wall.

'My mam comes in here crying every day now,' said Angela. She turned on the record player and put the needle on the record that was already on. A woman's voice came out but it wasn't anybody I knew. The song sounded really sad.

'She sleeps in here sometimes now. That's why the ashtray is here. The gardai searched everything looking for clues but I don't think they found anything. They took away her diary but then they brought it back. I think it was boring, just I did this, I did that.'

She was bent down now, fumbling at the wardrobe.

'Anyway, this is what I wanted to show you.'

She turned around and she was holding up a box that had a picture of four old lady's hands with huge rings hovering over a board with old fashioned letters printed on it. It said OUIJA MYSTIFYING ORACLE.

'It's an Ouija board.' She was whispering as if it was extra scary but I wasn't scared.

I asked her if it was the one they'd used when they had the séance in my house and she made her eyes go up and around and said that when they did it in my house they just wrote the letters on the floor with chalk and put a yes and a no and used a glass.

To be honest I still didn't like the whole thing about the séance in my house and Angela not telling me about it so I wasn't exactly thrilled to see the Ouija board. It kind of made me feel a bit like I didn't like Angela.

'Marion sent away to America for it,' she said. 'It came in the post.'

I didn't say anything. I just started looking at Marion's books. The only one I knew was The Godfather and that was because it was the one my father was reading before he died.

'I thought you'd be excited,' said Angela, sounding all disappointed. 'We could talk to the dead. You, me and Tony could do it.'

I was about to say that they didn't need an Ouija board when they did the séance in my house so what was the point but just then there was the sound of a car pulling into the driveway so I didn't actually say anything.

Angela's face changed.

'Quick! We shouldn't be in here.'

She shoved the Ouija board into the wardrobe and turned off the record player and we hurried back into her bedroom.

Timmy was still on the bed so I sat down beside him. His tail wagged a bit.

I could hear the sound of the front door being opened

then approximately ten seconds later it was slammed.

'It's them alright,' whispered Angela.

She was sitting right beside me and Timmy on the bed and you could tell she wasn't glad that they were back. Her hand was petting Timmy but the two of them were just staring at the door. Timmy's head was sideways a bit so he could hear better.

The voices downstairs sounded like they were arguing and I felt sorry for Angela then because I knew what it was like when my mother and father argued. They used to argue about him being in the pub all the time and, even though I knew that they did actually like each other, sometimes days would pass and they wouldn't be talking.

All of a sudden, her father's voice roared and bellowed through the house: 'GO TO HELL!'

'I'm already there, you dirty bastard,' screamed the mother.

Loads of plates or something got smashed on the floor and then it got really quiet for approximately forty seconds and then somebody went out the door and slammed it so hard the house shook. You could hear their feet on the gravelly driveway. Then the car started. The wheels went around really quickly and it zoomed off.

I imagined it squashing the squashed dog or fox even

more.

Everything went quiet again.

'I have to go downstairs,' said Angela. She had wet eyes. The bedroom door stayed open when she left.

I could hear the mother crying and Angela's feet going down the stairs.

I had a funny feeling in my stomach. I petted Timmy but he was too worried about what was going on and petting seemed like the last thing he wanted so I stopped.

I sat very still, hardly moving at all. I could hear myself breathing through my mouth and I could hear talking downstairs.

Then Timmy let out a whine and stood up and walked off the bed and out of the room. I could hear the nails on his paws go down the stairs, slowly, a step at a time.

I was by myself now.

I started brushing Timmy's hairs off the duvet for something to do. Pretty soon I had a little ball of hair. I wanted to learn how to knit but that was another thing for girls. I threw the ball of hair into the bin beside the chest of drawers. There was a scrunched up bit of paper with handwriting on it in the bottom of the bin. I bent down to get a closer look, wondering if this was Angela's poetry I'd found, when suddenly I got the feeling there was somebody behind me and the room got darker and colder.

I turned around, but there was nobody there, just me in the mirror.

I said hello, but the me in the mirror didn't say anything back. He looked at me, kind of worried.

I went closer to the mirror and jumped a bit without my feet actually leaving the ground. Just bending my knees and unbending them really fast. I was sort of shaking myself, but up and down instead of sideways.

I had breasts.

Sometimes I imagined a future when people were just heads floating around.

In the French Revolution they chopped peoples' heads off and the heads stayed alive for approximately fifteen seconds and they could see their bodies lying on the floor with blood pouring out of the neck and the crowds roaring and laughing at them. Marie Antoinette said let them eat cake before they chopped her head off but it did her no good when she found herself with her body chopped off, looking at the crowd roaring and laughing at her, and the blood pouring out of her neck where it used to be attached to the rest of her. No sirree, she was well and truly fucked.

I went back over to the bin and got the piece of paper out and unscrunched it. It was Angela's handwriting alright but it wasn't poetry, it was the beginning of a letter: *Dear Marion, I miss you. I wish you*

Writing letters to people didn't mean that you knew where they were or even that they were alive.

I knew that well enough.

I scrunched the paper back up and dropped it in the bin.

There was no sound in the entire house and I was starting to feel a bit like I should just go.

I listened hard for approximately ten seconds and I could hear really quiet crying downstairs and my mind suddenly made me think about this day just after my father died when my mother had a big row with my uncle Brian. They were arguing in the kitchen while me and Mrs Brown from down the landing were in the sitting room. She (i.e. Mrs Brown) was just visiting to say how sorry she was about my father when the row started.

I didn't understand what the row was about and I don't think Mrs Brown did either.

Anyway, next of all Mrs Brown just put her finger to her lips, pointed to the front door to tell me she was going (without actually speaking, not even her lips moving), and off she went. She just closed the door really quietly behind her.

Families don't want you around listening to them screaming and shouting at each other so I decided to copy Mrs Brown.

I put on my anorak.

I was singing the Gloria Gaynor song under my breath, just my lips moving, looking at myself in the mirror and thinking that I kind of looked like a spaceman with my hood up, when I noticed a photograph that had been there all the time, stuck in the corner of the mirror. My arm reached up to get it, slowly, like an actual spaceman, and pulled it off the mirror.

It was Angela and her family at the seaside. They were standing around in their swimming togs and they were all really slim. The father wasn't hairy, and he was taller than my father. The mother looked happy, not a bit like the lady downstairs. Angela was smiling. She had her arm around Marion's shoulder. It had to be Marion. She had navy blue girls' swimming togs. It wasn't a bikini. It had a little white skirt thing. Her hair was in a pageboy. The sky was blue. Judging by Angela, I'd say the photograph wasn't old. I thought about the girl who whizzed past on the bike, how she was a blur, how I could make her into anybody really. I wanted to see more photographs. I wanted to know exactly what Marion looked like. Maybe then I could tell if it was her on the bike. There had to be loads of photographs of her in the house. I wanted to see them all.

But then I heard somebody coming up the stairs so I stuck the photo back up and pulled my hood down. I was just standing there when Angela came back in, but she was too busy crying to notice anything about me and, to be honest, that made things even more weird.

It wasn't that I didn't realise how Marion going missing and Angela's mother and father shouting and screaming at each other wasn't important and terrible, it's just that I'd begun to see it all as a mystery, and now with Angela back and tears in her eyes and her lighting a cigarette under the window in the ceiling and me just not knowing what to do or say, well it made me feel even more useless and awkward.

'I hate this family,' said Angela. 'Everything always goes wrong.'

She had a drag, holding the cigarette in a funny way, like I'd seen rich women in films hold cigarettes.

'I wish I was never born,' she said.

A tear was staying in the same place on her cheek.

I didn't know what to say so I just said I was glad she was born because she was my friend.

The smoke wasn't going out the window like it was supposed to so she flapped her hands around for approximately five seconds. Then she took a little tiny bottle of whiskey out of her pocket and drank half of it and handed me the rest. I said no so she drank it all. She had the look I didn't like.

She passed the cigarette and I had a drag.

'You look like you're all having a great time in that

photo,' I said.

I was shaking my head up and down in the direction of the mirror. Smoke was coming out of my nose.

She took the cigarette out of my mouth, had a drag, and threw it out the window. I took the photograph off the mirror but she grabbed it off me.

She struck a match and lit the corner of the photo.

'I'm sick of this whole family.'

She dropped the burning photo in the bin. Funny smoke came out.

I didn't say anything. I felt depressed and I couldn't think of one thing that would make either of us feel any better. I knew we were friends of course but right then I didn't feel like we liked each other at all. Angela didn't look like she liked anybody or anything. Sometimes it can feel like people, even people you love, are out to get you and then that turns into the feeling that you're out to get them too.

But next of all Angela went over to the bed and got something out of her anorak and came back and handed it to me. It was the David Bowie tape. I'd forgotten about it. She'd written David Bowie in special writing and coloured in the letters.

I said thanks and she made her face smile so I smiled back.

Then I just said I was going and she said goodbye.

There was a lot of smoke in the room.

I went down the stairs carefully so they didn't creak. It was like the house was empty even though I knew Angela and her dog and the mother were all in there. I looked back at the house when I was outside and I made explosion sounds under my breath.

Then I got on the bike and started cycling but you can imagine my surprise when I got to the bit where the squashed dog or fox should have been *and it was gone*. There was a stain on the road but the actual dog or fox had disappeared.

It gave me the creeps so I cycled as fast as I could. I didn't stop at the pig shed. I didn't even look.

When I got back my mother was at home. I tried to put the bike under the stairs but it didn't fit so I put it in the shed. The washing machine was on. The noise of it meant you couldn't relax.

'I don't feel right, mam,' I said. And it was true. I had a headache and my throat hurt.

She made me go upstairs and change. I got straight into my pyjamas and that made me feel better.

When I was handing over the dirty clothes she put her hand on my forehead and left it there for approximately five seconds.

She said I felt hot and I was to have a hot drink before I went to bed. I went and got my book to read by the fire.

I sort of liked being sick.

Anyway, I was sitting there minding my own business and reading my book and trying to ignore the racket from the washing machine when all of a sudden, out of nowhere really, she asked me if I knew a lad called Tony Byrne.

She had to kind of shout because of the noise.

'He used to live in a caravan on the back roads.'

'Who?'

She said his name again, looking straight at me.

'No,' I said. 'I never heard of him.'

I put my head down as if I was reading my book.

The washing machine made a noise like a space ship taking off and zooming into the sky.

'The gardai are looking for him. They found that girl's bike buried in a garden and this lad was supposed to be doing nixers there and living in one of the workmen's huts. They're after searching a farm where he used to live as well.'

'I've just been up in Angela's,' I said. 'She didn't say anything about it.'

'Mr Daly told me,' she said.

I looked up from my book and I caught her looking at me like she knew I wasn't telling the truth, like she was thinking about me and wondering what I was really like and who I actually was.

Later on, I had stew but no bread for my tea and then I went upstairs and read my book on the bed with the superser on high. I couldn't really concentrate so I put the David Bowie tape on and got under the bed. I'd started to like David Bowie a lot. I stayed under there for the whole of one side but I had to come out to turn it over.

That night, before I went asleep, while I was sitting up in bed with my hot drink, I tried to imagine Marion's bedroom again, in every single detail, down to the smell of the perfume and talcum powder and the duvet and the carpet. I imagined opening her wardrobe and looking at all her coats and blouses and skirts and opening her drawers and seeing all her underwear and socks.

I didn't think about the Ouija board in the bottom of the wardrobe too much but I knew it was there.

I kind of tried to imagine being Marion and having Angela as my sister and Tony as my boyfriend and having a racer and spreading VD.

I tried to imagine what she was feeling and where she actually was but I could only think of her empty bedroom, all lonely and dark with the door closed, and light from the landing coming in under the door and light from the moon coming in the window in the ceiling, and the sounds outside of the rest of the family and them roaring and shouting at each other, and the pop stars in the posters on the wall staring down on the empty dark.

I thought about the letter to Marion in Angela's bin but I definitely didn't think it meant that Angela knew where Marion was. In a way, the letter was like a prayer and I said the prayer to my dead father as I was falling asleep: Dear father, I miss you. I wish you.

And when I did eventually fall asleep, I didn't have any dreams at all.

◆

The next morning, on the way back from mass, my mother told me I'd woken her up in the middle of the night shouting and screaming and when she came into my room to see what was going on I'd thrown all the covers off me in my sleep and she had to pull them back over me. She said that I looked like I was having loads of dreams and I was sweating a lot even though I felt cold when she touched my forehead.

I didn't like the idea of her being in my bedroom when I was asleep. I knew the rash was gone from the area but I still didn't want her looking at me when I was asleep. If I went into her bedroom when she was asleep and touched her it would be like being a burglar or a rapist or something, or at least that's what it would feel like to me, but she thought it was ok to be in my bedroom. It was just another one of those things about being the son.

Anyway, this particular Sunday, uncle Brian was coming around. It was ages since he'd come around so I wondered if there was something going on. He was my father's brother and the night my father died he actually gave me a hug. It was one of those things that happened, that had never happened before, and would never happen again. Well, maybe when my mother died it would happen again.

It all happened in the hospital.

I was in the corridor by myself and Brian had gone to the toilet. I was staring at this boy who was covered in plaster. He was all white. His father was holding him. He was like a doll. He must have broken every bone in his body. The corridor was the colour of custard. I was really hungry. I kept imagining my father with blood pouring out of him and his bike scrunched up beside him on the road and him just lying there maybe with his eyes hanging out of his head on stalks. I wanted to stop thinking about it but I didn't know how.

Somebody was crying somewhere.

I could hear all the different noises.

Brian was married to my aunt Susan who'd never hugged me either. She was with my mother inside in the little room. My mother had stopped screaming and crying. I wasn't sure what to do. I was just sitting there.

The lights were really bright. Brian came back from the toilet. He said he was going outside for a cigarette.

I got up and went with him. We didn't speak or anything. We were in a funny part of the hospital. It was dark outside. There was a tree lying down. We sat on it. Brian lit a cigarette. I didn't smoke then but I knew he would give me one if I asked. We were just quiet for a while. There was a plane in the sky and a few stars but no moon or clouds.

'Where will daddy be tonight?' I said.

I'd never seen any shooting stars although I knew they existed and they actually were tiny meteorites i.e. bits of rock from the far reaches of the universe entering our atmosphere and exploding.

'Your daddy will be in heaven,' said Brian.

'I don't mean that,' I said, 'I mean where will he be, will he stay in the hospital or will he be in our house in a coffin?'

Brian put his arm around my shoulder.

'I don't know, probably stay in the hospital,' he said.

And then he put his other arm around me. It was awkward because of the way we were sitting but I put my arms around him too. My eyes were wet. I could smell him. My face got stuck in his shoulder at the front under the neck. I didn't have a choice in any of this. I held onto him. I could feel him breathing really hard.

He smelled like my father. He was my father's brother. We were hugging each other. Salt water from my eyes went on his shirt. He was breathing hard. I was twisted around in a funny way. I prayed to God not to be bent. I had never hugged anybody like that before. I could smell him. I could smell cigarettes. My father's cigarette butts were in the ashtray at home. I wanted to smoke them. My father was good at smoke rings. He had veins like electric wires running up his arms.

Then Brian stopped hugging me and he never hugged me again. My aunt Susan came looking for him and we all went back inside.

At the funeral Brian didn't say one word to me and we didn't see much of him after the funeral. It was just my mother and me then.

Anyway, as I said previously, he was coming around and we were having roast chicken for dinner. I was actually mashing the potatoes when he arrived.

'Sure he'll make somebody a lovely wife someday,' said Brian.

He was talking about me. I pretended not to hear. He was my father's younger brother. The other brother was the eldest, the black sheep of the family. He lived in England and never even came to the funeral.

'Have you got a bird yet?' Brian said.

I said no.

Mash. Mash. Mash.

'Oh, he's got a girl calling around all the time now,' said my mother.

Mash. Mash. Mash.

I was sure that they were looking at each other, giving signals and making faces.

I finished the potatoes and put them back on the cooker to keep warm. Brian was cutting the chicken. I saw him gobbling down a big bit of chicken skin. He made a *sshhh* sign but I told my mother anyway and she gave out to him but we were all suddenly having a laugh and it made everybody feel better, and then my mother put out the plates and we all sat down and had our dinner.

Afterwards we went for a drive in the car. I sat in the front. I pushed the special lighter into the dashboard to light their cigarettes. Brian kept saying women drivers were no use and my mother and him started arguing but it was in a jokey way. We were all laughing but then I looked out the window and who did I see except RottingDead with FlanaganBrannigan on her back galloping into the sky over the hedges at the side of the road. The pair of them looked like they were having a great time and FlanaganBrannigan actually gave me a big wave before they galloped on ahead, fast as the wind, and out of sight. I had a quick look at Brian and my mother but they didn't look like they'd seen anything unusual so I said nothing.

We drove out to the sea and parked in a car park and went for a walk along the beach. It was cold and the sea was out so far you couldn't really see it and the sand stretched miles away. Birds took off and landed. You could hear their funny cries and the sky was the colour of pearls.

My mind made me think about this time when I was with my father on the beach and there was sand in the sandwiches and inside my mouth on my tongue and he had sand down his back from where he'd been in the sea and got wet and there was sand in my runners. He told me a joke and I couldn't stop laughing. He was a great swimmer and so was I even though I didn't like taking my clothes off in front of everybody. I told my mother this once when we were having a fight because I didn't want to go swimming with school and she went quiet and then she said I got the good swimming off my father and I got the not wanting to take my clothes off in front of everybody off of her. She never forced me to go swimming with school again.

Brian and my mother were walking ahead and talking all this time. They obviously had something important to discuss that wasn't for me to hear and I thought it was probably about my aunt Susan whose nerves were at her because she couldn't have a baby.

My mother was shaking her head up and down and being serious and Brian was making weird faces.

I liked my aunt Susan because she told me once that dreams were your real feelings from down inside you that you didn't really know you had. She had black hair that she wore in a pony tail. My mother didn't really like me talking about my dreams about my father but I knew she had dreams about him too, dreams that were driving her mad. I heard her dreaming in her bedroom in the middle of the night.

Aunt Susan told me you actually went mad if you didn't have dreams. She said if you had a dream about the sea it meant great change in your life like moving or getting married. I never dreamed about the sea but sometimes I could smell it even though I wasn't anywhere near it, and I could hear the waves and imagine all the fish and seaweed and bits of old boats and shells.

As I said previously, I would like to be burnt in a boat when I die, and then for my skeleton to sink into the sea, and then to drift around in the ocean for years and years and wash up on a beach miles away in another country and to have sea weed and shells stuck on me and a boy to find me who would hear the sea at night in his bedroom when he put his head on the pillow even though the sea was miles away. My skeleton would watch over him when he was asleep and make sea noises like waves breaking on beaches far away. The boy wouldn't be scared of me and I would glow in the dark.

Anyway, my mother and Brian had stopped walking and talking now and they were just standing there, looking at me as if I was supposed to say something.

'Is he deaf or something?' said Brian.

We were on the edge of the land. Nobody else was around.

'He lives in a dream world,' said my mother.

'I don't live in a dream world,' I said.

Of course, the truth was that I did actually live in a dream world, and my mother was right, but the reason why I was looking like I was living in a dream world at that very second was that I had just spotted RottingDead and FlanaganBrannigan out further than us, out where the water was silvery sparkles and the world turned into clouds.

'Come on,' said Brian, sounding annoyed. 'Get a move on! We're going to the pub.'

RottingDead and FlanaganBrannigan sort of disappeared. They were just sparkles on my eyes.

I turned around and we all started walking towards the road.

Uncle Brian looked a bit like my father and so I tried pretending that my father wasn't dead and it was him and me and my mother out for a walk and they were in love and we were all happy together.

Except things weren't actually like that when my father was alive. It was more just going to work and school and everything being the same as always, but with my father around and we didn't really go for walks at the seaside in winter. My father usually went to the pub on Sundays and then came home and had his dinner and went asleep. He was always tired from the overtime. He snored and farted while my mother and me watched the Sunday matinee. If he snored during a good bit my mother would dig him to make him stop and then he'd open and close his mouth and make a funny face and that always made us laugh and we'd miss the good bit anyway.

The pub was dark and smoky with show jumping on the telly. I didn't like golf or football or tennis or hurling or soccer or rugby or snooker or billiards or Gaelic football or crazy golf or handball or any other ball game. Your balls were your testicles and that was it as far as I was concerned. But I didn't mind show jumping or wrestling.

I had coke and a packet of cheese and onion and my mother had peanuts and a vodka and orange. Brian had a pint of Guinness.

'Ah, that's lovely,' he said, when he had his first mouthful. There was creamy stuff on his moustache.

'Men love their Guinness,' said my mother, making her eyes go up and around.

The night he died, my father drank three pints of Guinness. My mother told me this. She said the world was a cruel place and everybody found out eventually. The man in the car that killed my father certainly found out. I didn't know if he had a wife or a son or a daughter or if he'd had any Guinness. I just knew that he wrapped his car around a tree and died.

Brian was the one who was in the pub with my father before he got on the bike. He was the last person ever to talk to my father and now he was talking to me:

'Are you looking after your mam?'

We were in the corner of the pub. It was really quiet. The cigarette smoke was blue. There was a little bit of crisp floating in my coke. Tiny bubbles were coming to the top. I could actually hear and see ultra tiny explosions when they popped. My mother was in the ladies. The pub was nearly empty.

'We look after each other,' I said.

'Good man,' he said.

He said he was a bit worried about my mother, that she was lonely now that my father was gone. He asked me if I thought she was alright.

'I don't know,' I said.

I didn't want to say anything about her crying in the

bedroom at night. I didn't want to say anything about Mr Daly. My father always said that things should stay inside the family. But then I knew all about my aunt Susan not being able to have children and I knew Brian was family but I also knew my mother thought he was a bit of a messer. She didn't like it when my father went to the pub with him because they would always be late.

'She misses Daddy,' I said.

'You're the man of the house now so you have to look after her.'

I said nothing. I knew what the man of the house was and I wasn't that. I was the son.

'You're a good lad,' he said, but I didn't believe him and the look on his face said something else, it said he didn't know who I was at all, it said please don't be bent and useless.

Then I asked him what the name of the man who killed my father was, the one who was driving the car.

He looked at me funny.

He said he couldn't remember but he was an old fellow and he ran a bike shop over on the South Circular, then he elbowed me to shut up, and I looked up and my mother was coming back from the ladies.

She looked nice in her polka dot dress. She sat down and edged herself along the seat toward me.

'Those toilets could do with a clean,' she said.

'We'll have one more, Peggy, then we'll go,' said Brian.

I hadn't heard my mother's name in ages. It was a bit like a secret name, like Madame X or Peggy X or Madame Peggy X which made me the son of Madame Peggy X.

'Right you are,' said Madame Peggy X.

She gave him the money and off he went. She watched him talking to the barman at the bar, a funny smile on her face like she was thinking about something nice. She had the golden brooch on with the mother of pearl in the middle.

I got up then and went to the toilet. All the tables had red tops with green ashtrays. Everything was dark like it was night time and the bar was all lit up with little lights. You could see golden bottles of whiskey and brandy upside down. There was a man turning into mush. His eyeballs and face were melting onto the bar. Brian was chatting to him.

I went through the door that said MEN. The light was flashing on and off. It was another world in there, not a nice place. It had a bad smell and RottingDead and FlanaganBrannigan were floating around and hovering. They were staring at me like it was the most ordinary thing in the world to be there, as if they were just waiting for me to come in.

The back part of RottingDead was stuck through the

wall into the ladies' next door. Only about two thirds of her could fit in the men's.

The walls were painted pink and they had tiny pimples all over them. There was writing everywhere and the light was going on and off and water was squirting.

'What do the pair of you want?' I said.

'I want a packet of cheese and onion,' said Rotting-Dead.

The toilet was echoey so her voice sounded even more like a ghost in a horror film. FlanaganBrannigan made his eyes go up and around.

'You're always hungry,' he said.

His face actually looked even worse than before, nearly all the flesh was gone off his skull and his eyes were like golf balls with eyes painted on them, and his teeth were big and yellowy. He looked frightened and frightening at the same time.

The three of us sort of just stared at each other for approximately four seconds. Then FlanaganBrannigan got his cigarettes out and lit one. He descended a bit to give me one too. The match lit on the third go.

RottingDead whinnied.

I had a drag and FlanaganBrannigan ascended back up a bit.

I was thinking that ghosts shouldn't really eat or smoke because they don't actually exist but FlanaganBrannigan must have read my mind because he pointed out that he didn't actually inhale his cigarettes whereas RottingDead did actually seem to swallow the food and, yes, that was unusual for a dead horse.

'What does it feel like being a ghost?' I said.

'I don't know how to answer that,' he said. 'It's like everything has been taken away from you but you're still there. Like a tyre that's been punctured but somebody's still cycling.'

He looked sad but then he always looked sad, like something really terrible had happened to him and that's why he died.

And then it hit me. It hit me like a gigantic meteor smashing into my brain, like I remembered something I'd forgotten I always knew, like the meteor landed and planes crashed and buildings exploded and volcanos erupted and billions of people died screaming and crying in agony.

I knew who FlanaganBrannigan was.

I knew it like I knew my own name. I knew it as far down deep inside me as I could go.

I knew who he was and I looked at him and he looked at me and he had a drag on his cigarette and he started coughing, hovering backwards in little spurts, and the sound of water squirting out of the pipes was getting louder and louder and it was the sound of a car going really fast up a road to its appointment with death.

'You,' I said.

'It was an accident, son. I'm very sorry.'

'I'm not your son,' I said. 'Don't you ever call me your son.'

Then RottingDead ascended through the ceiling leaving me alone with FlanaganBrannigan. She must have known we needed to talk and it was private. I could see two of her hoofs sort of floating right up in the ceiling like funny lampshades or something but it didn't make me think about atoms or things turning into mush or bodies moving through brick walls and I wasn't thinking about my father as a tree trunk with one nail hammered into him and a trickle of blood coming out and I wasn't thinking about what it's like in the cold grave with only spiders for company.

No sirree, I wasn't thinking about any of those things.

What I was thinking about was the car going up the road and the bike going up the road and the two of them had their appointment with death, and the almighty crash and the screaming and shouting pouring out of the car, and my father flying and doing somersaults, and FlanaganBrannigan, in his car wrapped around the tree, with blood pouring everywhere and screams of agony and horror coming out of him.

My father died in less than a second. Less than a

millionth of a second. No screaming. He was dead when he hit the ground.

It was FlanniganBrannigan, the murderer of my father, who died screaming in agony, screaming and crying with his eyes hanging out of his head on stalks and blood gushing and squirting everywhere.

I had a long drag on my cigarette, right down deep inside me it went. It made me feel better. It was suddenly quiet, quiet as if it had been noisy for years and then that noise had stopped and you couldn't believe that things could ever have been noisy before.

FlanaganBrannigan's ugly face was staring right into my eyes.

'Your father died right away,' he said.

Tears started coming out of my eyes and rolling down my cheeks.

'Were his eyes hanging out of his head and was he screaming in agony?' I said.

'No, his body was still there but he, the man who was your father, was gone straight away. In less than a millionth of a billionth of a second. I know it sounds funny but you could call it a peaceful death even though it was sudden and violent.'

'Why are you here then, when my father isn't?'

'I'm not sure,' he said, and he sounded really, really tired of everything.

'Do you have a wife and children?'

'No.'

'Well I don't want you around so why don't you go and fuck off,' I said, and, as soon as I said it, Flanagan-Brannigan started to dissolve into grey smoky stuff. It started with his mac and then his feet and his hands and the raggedy looking clothes that he had on under the mac. All of it sort of lost its shape a bit and sort of floated off into nothing. It was like he was a big smoke ring in the shape of a man and a little breeze had come from somewhere and blown him away.

He ended up with just his skull floating in the air and his big bulging eyes looking at me, and they did look sad and maybe I even felt sorry for him, and then only his big yellowy teeth were left and they just said Sorry again and then they disappeared altogether as well, and the sound of the word *sorry* kind of lost its shape as if it had never been said in the first place and anyway, as my father used to say, sorry is no good when the damage is done.

And then I was alone in the toilets by myself and the light went off and on a few more times and then it stayed off but it was just bright enough to see what I was doing.

I had the last drag on the cigarette and threw it in the toilet and I took out my penis and urinated on it. A lot of urine came out. There was little yellow roundy things in the toilet too. They had a lemony smell. My heart was beating. The rash Down Under was completely gone and the area was no longer itchy and red.

I put my penis away and turned around and RottingDead was back. She took up the whole space and her back part kept disappearing into the wall.

She didn't say anything. She just kept looking at me. One of her eyes was gone. It was a black hole. Out of the black hole came one tear. It was silver and it rolled down the side of her head but it didn't fall off.

'Why are you so sad, RottingDead?'

'Because boys did this to me.'

'But I'm a boy,' I said.

She didn't say anything. The tear fell off. You could sort of see through her. Time was slowed down. It was like she was there but she wasn't there. She was where my father was and where my dead sister was. She was down in the grate in the cold Winter mornings. She was the atoms all around me every day of my life. She was being hungry and never being full even when I was so full I actually felt sick. She was my mother crying at her dressing table at night. She was a feeling in my stomach I didn't know but I felt it all the same, especially at night, especially in my bedroom, especially when tears were coming right out of my eyes and actually landing on the floor.

'Hold out your hand,' said RottingDead.

I held out my hand.

And RottingDead began to change. She began to shrink down to her atoms. She stopped being see through. The back of her wasn't sticking through the wall anymore. She ascended a bit. She was a flying horse. She opened her beautiful wings. You couldn't see through her anymore. Her wings were a mixture of colours. She descended a bit. She was just hovering. She got even smaller. She was a little thing. I could feel the little breezes. She was like a horse a doll would own. Her feet were tiny. She landed on my hand. She weighed hardly anything at all.

'Now pull up your shirt,' said RottingDead, and her voice wasn't from a horror film anymore.

I pulled up my shirt with my free hand. I looked down at my stomach. It wasn't my usual stomach. It wasn't the stomach I hated. I could see inside this stomach. There was a little cage there. There was a little mirror with a little bell on it. There was a little pile of cheese and onion in the corner. The bars of the cage made a funny sound. The bars slid sideways like the door of a spaceship.

I looked at RottingDead, except it wasn't RottingDead anymore.

Magic had actually happened.

RottingDead was gone and Bluey was back.

Bluey opened his beautiful wings. Bluey chirped. Bluey said, 'Who's a pretty boy then?'

I am, Bluey, I am.

Bluey was home. Bluey cheeped. Bluey opened his beautiful wings. Bluey was all blue. I was happy Bluey was back. I was proud of Bluey. I told Bluey I loved him. Bluey said chirpychirpycheepcheep.

I put Bluey inside in his cage. I put Bluey back inside me. Bluey said, 'Who's a pretty boy then?'

I am, Bluey, I am.

The bars of the cage made a funny sound. The bars of the cage closed like a spaceship. Bluey looked up at me from his perch. Bluey was happy to be home. I put my finger to my lips to tell Bluey to be a bit quiet.

Bluey said ok.

Bluey hopped down to his little pile of cheese and onion. Bluey started to munch. Bluey was home. Bluey started to crunch.

I tucked my shirt back in. I looked normal again. Nobody would ever know. I went to the sink. I looked in the mirror. The light came on again. It wasn't my face in the mirror. The face of my father looked back at me from the mirror. The face of my father was smiling. He was kind of just hovering. He had his crown on. He said not to worry, that he was still the man of the house. He looked like he was ok really. Then he said goodbye. He sort of disappeared.

My face came back.

I smiled a monster smile. Water started squirting.

I washed my hands and went back out of the toilets. Everything was normal. Brian was still talking to the man at the bar. The man was still turning to mush. The show jumping was still on. My mother was still lighting a cigarette. It lit on the first go. The smoke was all blue. Her feet weren't touching the floor. She was like a little girl. I wanted to be able to stop her crying in her bedroom but I couldn't.

I slid along the seat towards her. The seat was ripped and you could see the spongey filling.

'What were you doing in the toilet for so long?' she said.

'What do you think?' I said.

'You were smoking, weren't you,' she said. 'I can smell it.'

Smoke was coming out of her nose when she said this.

'You're only smelling yourself,' I said.

Brian came back with the drinks. He was able to hold all the drinks at the same time. He had nuts in his pockets.

'I hope the pair of you aren't arguing,' he said, setting down the glasses and throwing the nuts on the table. He gave the pair of us a funny look. His eyes went from me to my mother then back but neither of us said anything.

We opened our nuts. I was lost in thought. I was thinking about my father. I wanted to ask my mother the name of the man who killed him even though I knew that it was Flanagan or Brannigan or something, even though I'd only been talking to the ghost of FlanaganBrannigan, the very man, a few minutes ago. I just wanted to hear my mother say his name. I wanted everybody to say the name of the man who killed my father. Even the nuns' and priests' heads in their cardboard boxes would say it. But I knew that wasn't going to happen and I knew I couldn't ask my mother questions like that, anyway, and I knew my mother wouldn't want to say his name. I knew everybody wanted everything to be ok and that meant not talking about my father rotting in his grave or saying the name of the man who killed him or talking about ghosts or boys chopping off horses' heads and exploding snakes and blood squirting everywhere and people roaring and crying with their eyes hanging out of their heads on stalks, and girls disappearing into nowhere and boys whose mothers and fathers just want them to be normal but they turn out to be bent and they never get married or have children even though they actually like girls, just not in a penis hardening way.

Anyway, I sat there for a while, just looking at the way

the smoke moved around in the air, thinking all of these things, and smelling the pub with its black stools and chairs and red tables and green ashtrays and all the blue smoke floating around and folding into the smell of my mother's perfume which she must have put on when she was in the toilet because I didn't notice it before then, and all of this added up to me being kind of hypnotised and not really thinking about anything at all and not really listening to anything at all, and then after a while of this I saw Brian with his head looking up at the ceiling, and his pint glass nearly upside down, trying to get the very last drop of Guinness to slide down into his mouth, and I could actually see what was left of the creamy head slipping down into his lips and that's how I knew it was time to go.

We all put on our jackets but I didn't put my hood up. Brian shouted thanks very much to the barman. The car park was empty and the sky was grey. The world sounded like the sound was actually turned down. The buildings were squashed by the sky. Cars whizzed past. On the other side of the road was the wet brown sand stretching for miles. The sea was invisible sparkles. Birds were flying.

'That was one of your dad's favourites. He always loved the pint in there,' said Brian. I looked back at the pub.

'Men,' said my mother, and the way she said it made it

obvious that she thought all men were thick. She made her eyes go up and around too.

When she just got in the car, it went down a few inches. The same must have happened when I got in, then Brian got in and it probably went down the least for him because he was the slimmest, and off we went.

◆

It didn't take Brian long to drive us home and we'd actually set the fire before we went out so we just needed to put a match to it when we got in. We had a cup of tea and a sandwich and then Brian went home. The fire got warmer and warmer. I didn't have any biscuits. My mother read her book and I read the paper.

Dear Valerie's problems were sort of boring. A woman was having sex with her husband's friend and Valerie said to stop. My mother and father didn't really have friends so I didn't think the problem would have come up for them. Now, of course, there was Mr Daly. I wanted to ask about him but I knew I couldn't.

'I can't be bothered with this bloody book.'

It was my mother. She stretched and yawned, holding the book up in the air, and then she just let it drop on the floor. It was *Wuthering Heights*.

'It just goes on and on,' she said.

I said a lot of stuff we had to do at school was like that.

She got up out of the armchair and turned on the telly. Her polka dot dress was all caught up and you could see her slip and see the blue veins in her legs.

There was an ad for all the special programmes and films that would be on over the Christmas. A Christmas tree with sparkly tinsel and ornaments on it had a different programme inside each ornament. They were singing White Christmas and my mother joined in and then I joined in too. We kept singing after the ad was over. She danced across to the sideboard and got out a big box of Christmas cards and waved them in the air and we ended up writing all the cards and having a sing song. It was the first sign of Christmas we'd had and it put us in a good mood for the rest of the night.

Then just before we were going to bed Angela phoned. My mother was filling the hot water bottles so I got it. She said her father hadn't been home since he left in the car when I was there. She was worried something bad had happened to him, that he was dead or something. They were checking the hospitals. Her mother was crying all the time and everything was horrible.

'The gardai were here earlier,' she was whispering. 'They found Marion's bike. The one she ran away on.'

'Where was it?' I said, even though I already knew.

'In a garden near where Tony was staying. He's done a

runner.'

'Do you know where he is?'

'Yeah.'

'Where?'

'Meet me tomorrow night, six o' clock, the back of Clonduff House, where the pond is.'

Click. She was gone.

'Who was that?' said my mother.

'Nobody.'

'Didn't sound like nobody to me.'

'Look, it's none of your business who phones me.'

'Don't be so cheeky.'

'I'm going to bed,' I said, but under my breath I was thinking fuck off fuck off fuck off over and over again.

Upstairs, the superser was glowing. I looked out the window for approximately four minutes at all the empty gardens and the windows with their lights on. One of the windows actually had Christmas lights up already. I felt the opposite of depressed. Then I put on the David Bowie tape really low and did my exercises. When the tape was over I just stayed where I was and listened to the wind blowing outside. Then I got into bed and went straight asleep.

◆

The next morning was really stormy. Rain was lashing

against the window. My mother said she'd been awake half the night listening to the wind whistling through the house. I cleaned the grate out and set the fire for when we got home. The radio said trees had fallen down and people down the country had no electricity. A boy got killed in his own bed. It was the last day before Christmas holidays.

The bus was packed and everybody was wet and the windows were all steamed up. I kept my hood up. There was trouble with girls screaming and shouting at each other. The bus conductor had to tell them off.

Pauline and Paul were sitting a few seats back and I heard them saying something about Angela's bent boyfriend i.e. me. I just got out my book about rats attacking civilisation and kept staring at it, pretending to read but not actually taking the words in. They kept saying Angela's bent boyfriend really loud and laughing so I'd definitely hear and know it was me they were talking about.

At lunchtime I went into town and bought my mother a scarf and gloves and a Christmas box of chocolates in Roches Stores. I hid them in my school bag so other boys wouldn't see them.

Then after lunch I got called to the office by the English teacher, Mr Murphy. He had a beard and glasses. He'd given us a really boring essay on what season of the year we liked the most and I'd done it on winter.

I knew I hadn't done anything terrible or been in trouble for a while so I wasn't worried and I actually liked walking around the school when everybody else was in their class.

He was sitting behind his desk and he had the light on even though it was bright enough and there was silvery rain running down the window. You could see the grey sky outside. The light inside in the room was sort of golden.

He said to sit down. The seat looked like old skin and I thought to myself that that is exactly what leather is made of i.e. old skin off dead animals, and then I sat down. The chair creaked and you could hear the clock ticking all the time.

He took my essay book out of his drawer.

'Another good essay here, John, a very good effort.'

He pushed the essay book towards me. I said thank you.

'Thank you, Sir,' he said.

I said it again with Sir on the end, and then we looked at each other for approximately seven seconds trying to read each other's minds. I looked away first.

'Your writing has improved. However I'm surprised by some of the things you're writing about these days.'

I moved around in the chair to try and get in a more

comfortable position. The creaks were really loud.

'Sorry, Sir,' I said.

'What are you saying sorry for?'

'I don't know.'

'I don't know, Sir,' he said.

I said it again with Sir on the end.

He smiled so I smiled back. Then the smile disappeared, and he opened the essay book and took out three folded up pages of foolscap. He unfolded them and I saw what they were and then I knew what this was all about and I got scared because what he was holding up was actually the story of RottingDead and FlanaganBrannigan.

I must have left it in the book when I gave in my essay and he must have read it. There were things in it that would get me into trouble, things that somebody like me wasn't supposed to be writing about.

I thought about all of this really quickly and, in the end, I couldn't see a way out because basically I thought it would be stupid to say I didn't write it, and, in anyway, a part of me was glad I'd written it and didn't care what Murphy or anybody else said. That part of me was the writer, and the writer wasn't afraid of anything, but then there was another part of me, the normal part, that knew I was in big trouble, and that part of me was actually quite worried.

'I think we can honestly say that you let your imagination

run away with you in this piece.'

He pushed the sheets toward me.

I said nothing for approximately eight seconds, just looked at the desk. The rain was lashing down and the clock was ticking like a bomb. I listened to the gaps between the ticks.

'Do you know what pornography is, John?' he said.

I said no sir even though I did know what it was. I'd seen pictures of women kissing each other in a magazine I found in the park. They had lipstick and eye shadow on, and they were wearing special underwear. They didn't look like any women I actually knew.

'Well, for a lad who doesn't know what pornography is, aren't you after doing a grand job of writing it,' he said, and then didn't he pick up the sheets of paper, the sheets of my story that I had written, and didn't he start tearing them in half right in front of me, and the sound the paper made was really loud, and the clock stopped ticking and the wind stopped blowing and the rain stopped lashing and all I could hear was the sound of this paper tearing, and all I could see was this mad look on his face, and his eyes kept going from the story he was tearing in half and back to me and back again to the story, and maybe he could see how shocked I was and how I looked like I wanted to kill him and it scared him or something because he actually stopped tearing and he looked at me really hard for approximately three seconds as if he was about to say something, and what did I do just then except reach over and grab the story of RottingDead and FlanaganBrannigan right out of his hands, yes sirree, and I actually said sorry, sir after I grabbed it, even though I wasn't sorry, I was just nervous, and then I got up out of the chair and I don't think the chair creaked this time and I was holding the story of RottingDead and FlanaganBrannigan behind my back and for a second we just looked at each other and then I walked backwards away from the desk, and he said nothing at all, and I just walked backwards to the door, and then he said you'll regret this when I have your mother down to this school and he was starting to stand up out of his chair and I still didn't say anything, and I opened the door and I walked out and he was shouting something and I just walked quickly down the corridor and I didn't look back, I just didn't stop until I got to the toilets and they were empty and quiet and I pushed in one of the doors and it made a huge bang and I sat down on one of the special toilet pots that were made for very small boys.

My heart was beating. My heart was beating. My heart was beating.

I sat on the little toilet pot and I wanted Mr Murphy to be hung, drawn and quartered and people to be roaring and laughing at him when he died in agony. I sat on the little toilet and I wanted to be the executioner dressed like a wrestler and holding Mr Murphy's head by the hair and showing him the rest of his body lying on the ground and blood gushing out of his fucking neck. I sat on the little toilet and I wanted an earthquake to come and for the school to fall down and for the bricks to run up the road screaming that there's no such thing as God and the only person to survive to be me and the story of RottingDead and FlanniganBrannigan to be in my pocket. I sat on the little toilet and I wanted a fire to burn the place to the ground and only me to live and the story of RottingDead and FlanniganBrannigan to be in my pocket. Then I wanted a plane to crash into the building and everybody to die screaming and shouting in a huge explosion except me and the story of RottingDead and FlanniganBrannigan to be in my pocket, and I was beginning to be ok, and I actually had a look at at the story of RottingDead and FlanniganBrannigan and I knew that I really liked it now and I was really glad that I wrote it.

It was torn in half and then those halves were torn again i.e. quarters but you could still stick it all back together and I really liked that story. It was exciting and I wrote it and now I wanted to go home and read it again and I wanted to write more of it.

I stood up. I folded up the parts that made up the story of RottingDead and FlanniganBrannigan and shoved it all down into my underpants. I opened the cubicle door. It was a bit dark and there was a brown stain on the ceiling from where Mr Brennan murdered a boy in the chemistry lab. I washed my hands and threw water on my face. I looked in the mirror. My teeth were pointy. Vampires actually existed i.e. people who sucked blood. I put my face right up close to the glass and looked right into my very own eyes. For the first time in my life I really saw that they were green. I already knew because Angela told me but I'd never actually spent time looking at them, really looking right into them.

They had silvery green sparkles in them, like glass marbles made of human flesh, and it was exciting to actually imagine my brain, like one of those crabs that lives in shells it finds lying around, hiding in there, behind the eyes, doing all the thinking about what was going to happen next, knowing that its job was to make sure that none of the teachers got their hands on the story of RottingDead and FlanaganBrannigan, knowing that there was trouble ahead and that I was bent and that I had a good imagination, and that I was going to be a writer when all this trouble was over and done with, but that maybe that was ages away.

Then I stopped looking in the mirror and I dried my

hands and face. I went out of the toilets and I walked to the stairs and I went down to the next floor where my class was. I was the only person on the stairs. You could hear my footsteps all through the building. I walked along the corridor to the classroom. Rain was lashing against the window panes. Somewhere I could hear a class singing a hymn but that was very far away and I didn't know what hymn it was but I knew it sounded holy. Then I was actually at the door of my classroom and I knocked on it and then I opened it.

Gorman, the history teacher, was writing stuff on the blackboard and the class was copying it down. All of this was normal and ordinary. Rain was lashing against the window panes. He didn't stop writing when I opened the door but when I sat down at my desk he suddenly announced that I was to stay behind to see him after class. He didn't turn around to look at me when he said this or even stop writing. You could hear the chalk on the blackboard and everybody was really quiet and just looking down at the copy books they were writing in.

Everybody that is except Liam Kelly.

He looked straight over at me and made his lips go into a big kiss.

I hated him but, for some reason, I couldn't be bothered worrying about him even a little bit anymore.

I could feel the story of RottingDead and Flanagan-

Brannigan in my underpants and that was the only important thing now.

I pretended to write what was on the board but I just drew circles inside circles inside circles like you were looking into little tunnels.

Then the bell went and all the boys started heading for the door.

I stayed where I was, looking at the desk but actually I was looking through the tops of my eyes and I could see that Murphy had come into the class and he was talking to Gorman.

This didn't surprise me but what did surprise me was I could feel the amount of hate I had for the pair of them get even bigger than it already was (which was gigantic).

When the last boy was finally gone there was silence for approximately five seconds. I kept looking down but pointing my eyeballs up so I could see what was going on at the front of the class. They were making faces and whispering about me for approximately another five seconds and then Gorman left and only Murphy was left. I could hear boys outside the class but the noise of them was getting quieter as everybody started to go home.

'Well, well, well,' said Murphy.

I looked up.

'What do you think your mother is going to think when she finds out that her son is writing filthy stories instead of doing his schoolwork?'

'I don't know, Sir.' I said. 'And, Sir, I don't care.'

He went from looking extremely annoyed to looking like he was going to explode and there'd be just bits of teacher everywhere, all over the walls, and stuff on my face that I'd have to wipe off, i.e. goo from inside him that got shot out in the explosion and splattered all over me.

'Come up here, you little bastard,' he said.

I kind of sighed in a cheeky way and started to get up.

'MOVE!' He flung a piece of chalk in my direction. It whizzed past my ear.

I walked up to the top of the class. I didn't take my eyes off him. His face was all red. I didn't have a bad feeling in my stomach.

'Hold out your hand,' he said.

I held out my hand. He raised his ruler up in the air. I looked into his eyes and he looked into mine. He could see that I hated him. He brought his ruler down on my hand. And it stung. It stung loads and loads and I closed my eyes and I saw a red alien sky filled with millions of exploding stars and approximately seven seconds passed but each of those seconds felt very, very long and when I opened my eyes I knew, I knew in my heart, that he could hit me as much as he wanted, he could hit me all day and all night, but he still couldn't win. He could never fucking win.

'Other hand.'

He got me on the fingers this time and I was in agony. I clamped my eyes shut and jumped out of my space ship and I fell through the red alien sky into the blood red sea and under I went, and I put my hands under the armpit of the arm belonging to the opposite hand, and up I came for air, and I opened my eyes and I looked at him and I told him the truth, in a calm voice first, and everything went quiet for approximately four seconds, and then I screamed the truth at him as loud as I could, as loud as I'd ever screamed anything in my entire life: 'YOU FUCKING MAKE ME SICK, YOU BASTARD!!!'

And then he was standing over me and trying to hit me anywhere he could but I was waving my arms around over my head to stop him, so he kept hitting my arms in different places, and then somehow, and I'm not really sure how I actually did it, I just kind of got away from him, and I ran out of the classroom and down the corridor and down the stairs and into the yard and out the gate, and all the time I was running I was actually thinking that I wanted to get home and listen to the David Bowie tape and read the story of RottingDead and FlanniganBrannigan again and maybe write some more of it or improve it or something and that was all I wanted, all I wanted in the whole wide world, and I never wanted to go to school ever again until the day I died.

I stopped running when I got around the corner at the top of the street. It was the furthest I'd run in ages and I was actually breathing really hard. I didn't have my coat or my school bag with me but I could feel the story of RottingDead and FlanniganBrannigan in my underpants and that was the important thing. I checked in my pocket and I had the bus fare home. That was lucky because usually I kept it in the secret pocket in my schoolbag.

The bus came really fast and, as soon as I was sat down on it, I took the story of RottingDead and FlanniganBrannigan out of my underpants and read it again. On the whole, I liked it but there were bits that were better than other bits, and bits that needed to be changed.

I missed my stop because I was concentrating so hard on reading but we lived only one stop before the terminus so that wasn't so bad.

The clock in the hall said it was a quarter to four. My mother wouldn't be home until six. I turned on the radio for company but it was just about sports and politics so I turned it off again. I made a banana Slender and drank it really fast and then I went upstairs and I got under the bed.

I had just made myself comfortable when the phone rang downstairs.

It was creepy, listening to it ring through the house and me not moving, like I wasn't really there, and the house was actually empty. It was a bit like being dead in your grave and having your family visiting your tombstone. It rang and rang and rang and then it stopped. I was sure it was the school, and even when it was stopped and the house was quiet again, the sound of it hung around in the air like it was always going to be there waiting and ringing, waiting and ringing for eternity.

Eventually I got out from under the bed and went downstairs and unplugged the phone at the wall to make sure it wouldn't ring again. My mother would never notice because the socket was behind the sideboard and it wasn't like the phone was always ringing or anything. That solved the problem of the school calling for that day and the next day was the beginning of the Christmas holidays so that was alright. I put the phone to my ear for a little while to make sure that it was dead and I could actually hear the wind blowing on a deserted planet millions of miles away in another dimension or something.

Then I pushed the furniture all to one end of the kitchen and I rolled the lino back. I'd been meaning to do this for a while.

There was all bits of dirt and mush everywhere under it. You think your kitchen is clean but just underneath everything is the mush and the dirt. I pushed everything back and it was actually there. I didn't think it would be but it was. Most of the letters were gone and you wouldn't notice it unless you were looking for it. The letters G, H, I, J , then a gap, then M, N, then a gap, then the word NO.

It was the Ouija board Marion, Angela and Tony had drawn on the floor all that time ago.

It was all true.

I rolled the lino back and put all the furniture back and then went back upstairs and climbed into my grave under the bed. All I had in the grave was the torch, an old microscope in a dusty box, the torn up pages of my story and my old slippers but I felt comfortable. That was enough for me.

I must have dropped off, because the next thing I knew my mother was coming in the front door. That meant it was nearly six, time to meet Angela.

I heard her close the front door, and her voice calling to see if I was in. It was hard not to answer your own mother but I had no choice.

I listened to her going around the house without me.

She was humming a song and it took me a while to figure out what song it was but when I did I nearly went right downstairs and had it out with her there and then.

It was the Kate Bush song and *she knew all the words.*

I actually couldn't believe my ears. She hated Kate Bush and now here she was singing the song. I managed to stay where I was even though I was angry and only when she'd stopped moving around and I couldn't hear her humming anymore I came out from the grave.

Very quietly, I got my old raincoat out of the wardrobe and put it on. It was the first time I'd worn it in ages. It didn't have a hood or anything. I snuck out the front door. It wasn't raining and there was no boys around.

◆

It was cold and misty and the back wall of Clonduff House was like a dark curtain hanging out of the sky. The bushes and trees whispered in the wind, and there was little bits of wool hanging off the thorns and wolves howling.

I sat down on a tree lying on its side and waited.

All my smoke rings fell apart and Angela didn't come.

Somebody opened one of the high windows in Clonduff House, one of the windows on the floor that had no stairs going up to it, and I saw a light flicker, and for a second, a figure at the window.

But Angela didn't come.

I had sparkles in my eyes, a candle at the highest window, always when I looked away. A little animal ran through the bushes. It was creepy, dead creepy, but I waited.

And I waited.

And no sign of Angela.

It wasn't like her. I must have waited a whole hour, probably longer. Time went funny. It wasn't like Angela. I was worried. It was a feeling in my stomach. I was freezing cold.

Later the gardai asked me loads of questions about what I actually did when I was waiting for her. But the truth was I did nothing. I just sat there and smoked. I was freezing cold and I was worried. I blew smoke rings. She was my best friend. I told the gardai that I loved Angela and never wanted anything bad to happen to her, and they said how did I know something bad had actually happened to her. They were full of traps and tricks. It was a bad time.

But I did eventually give up waiting and I did go home. I had to. I couldn't wait forever. It was lonely.

My mother was actually in. She was watching telly and doing the ironing, happy enough, so I just said hello and went upstairs.

I put the superser on and listened to the David Bowie tape really low under the blankets in my socks and pyjamas.

I don't really remember much else about that night except a weird dream I had:

I was in the farmhouse on the back roads. It was a mixture of the farmhouse, the caravan and the upstairs room in Clonduff House, the one that had no stairs going up to it. I knew it was a mixture of these rooms even though I'd never been in any of them. The place had been ransacked and everything was all over the place and banjaxed. The table and chair legs were sticking up in all directions and the curtains were rotten and the windows were filthy. All the cushions had their insides hanging out and the wallpaper was mouldy and peeling off.

There was a crown on the ground, under a pile of old newspapers. It was the same crown my father wore, the one like the little pin cushion in the china cabinet downstairs in the real world, except it was bigger and you could actually wear it. It was the colour of the roses on a boy's birthday cake. It had a little measuring tape you could pull out. I wanted to measure how tall I was so I put the crown on my head and started to pull the measuring tape out. Then the door opened and the two farmers came in. One of them was actually the coalman but he was covered in muck, not coal. The other one was just a normal farmer. It was like two farmers and one farmer at the same time. They were climbing over the furniture trying to get at me. There was an old mattress on the floor and I tripped over it and they got me and grabbed me by the hair. They were pushing my face into the mattress. It was all stained. My crown came off. I was in my stocking feet. They were right on top of me. I could hardly breathe.

When I woke up I was sweating and my penis was hard. It was the middle of the night and I could hear my mother crying next door in her bedroom.

I don't know why but it all just struck me as really funny.

I couldn't help it. There was a monster inside me. I was breaking my heart. I lay in the bed laughing my head off. Every time I stopped I'd hear my mother crying in her bedroom, and that would start me off again. After a while I masturbated. The area was fine. I kept bursting out laughing, breaking my heart. Then I'd masturbate again. Then I'd be laughing. Then I'd masturbate. I thought about the coalman during the masturbation. I used Nivea.

◆

The next morning was bad. My mother woke me shouting at me about the telephone and running out of school and being with bad teenagers, and what had gone wrong with me, and then she started crying and saying she tried her best but it was never good enough, and where was my father when she needed him, and he was hopeless anyway, and everything was always left to her, and she'd had enough, and on and on she went and then she kind of slipped down the wall in my bedroom and ended up sitting on the floor crying with her arms flapping around.

I lay in the bed looking at her until she was just atoms and everything was floating around in the mush and I decided the best thing to do was to say nothing at all.

I turned around in the bed and faced the wall.

Eventually I heard her get up off the floor and go downstairs.

It was the worst I'd ever been to my mother, ignoring her like that, but I didn't feel bad about it, just kind of empty. I watched the wall turn into mush in front of my eyes, and in the back of my head I was trying to think of nothing, but it didn't really work because my mind kept making me think about just after my father died and he was buried and everything, and the funeral was over and everybody was gone and things were supposed to be sort of normal again, but they weren't, and one of the ways in which they weren't normal was that whenever my mother said anything to me, I kept thinking she was going to cry even though she had no actual tears in her eyes. So I kept finding myself looking into her eyes really hard even though I didn't want to.

And I kept thinking that she was looking into my eyes really hard too to see if I was going to cry.

It made talking to each other complicated, it made me want to look away all the time, it made me feel like we were seeing into each other's souls and neither of us wanted to but we couldn't stop.

Then one night she was lying on the sofa reading her book and I was on the floor reading mine, it was just a few days after the funeral, and we were saying nothing, and the telly and the radio and the record player were all switched off. It was dead quiet, and it was like that for ages, and then all of a sudden my mother announced that, from now on, I'd have to clean the budgie's cage since my father was dead and gone so he couldn't do it.

It takes a while to realise all the things the dead father used to do, that won't be getting done anymore, and this was just one of them.

I didn't say anything. I didn't really want to talk much ever again.

But then the next morning, when my mother went to the shops, I took Bluey's cage down and actually started to clean it. He was allowed to fly around once the window was closed. I just meant to clean the cage and him to have a fly around and me to put him back in and everything to be ok. But that wasn't what happened. What happened was that I opened the window really wide and chased Bluey around, flapping my arms and screaming and shouting, until he flew out the window.

I shouted as loud as I could, like I was possessed by the devil, and my throat was raw and tears were coming out of my eyes.

I think I actually wanted to kill Bluey but, in a way, it was like I was afraid of Bluey. It was like I was afraid of everybody and everything.

When my mother came back from the shops, I told her that it was an accident and I even cried a bit but she said she didn't mind that Bluey was gone, that she was just glad that I was alright and that we had each other to look after now, and I said yes I know but I didn't really know, I was only pretending I knew.

I didn't want to look after her. I didn't want to look after anybody. Not even Bluey.

My mother said to keep the cage because we might want another budgie eventually but I definitely didn't want to get another budgie, not ever, and, I didn't think she did either.

Anyway, the reason why I was thinking about all this was because, lying there facing the wall and ignoring my mother, I was slowly beginning to realise something, and the something I was slowly realising was that I actually wasn't that afraid anymore, definitely not as afraid as I was when my father died, no sirree, and maybe even less afraid than I'd ever been in my entire life.

I felt kind of empty alright, but the empty feeling was fair enough because when something is empty it can be filled up again and that sort of made being empty ok.

I don't mean that I thought everything was fine. That would be impossible. I just knew that things were different in a good way. I wasn't even sure what was good about them yet.

And that's why I looked at the wallpaper for five whole hours.

My mother came in twice and said things but I didn't listen and I didn't say anything and she just left again but I knew five hours had passed because next of all somebody came into my bedroom and I thought it was my mother again but it wasn't, it was Mr Daly.

'Your mother says you've been up here for five hours,' said Mr Daly's voice.

I didn't turn around.

'I brought you some photos to look at,' said Mr Daly. I said nothing. I was thinking why did he bring photos for me. I could hear bits of paper rubbing off each other.

'It's the original family who lived in Clonduff House. I got them in the cottage on the old farm. I was helping the niece do a clear out.'

'How come you know everybody around here?' I said.

'I'm nosy,' he said.

I turned away from the wallpaper and faced Mr Daly.

'Do you have a wife and children?' I said.

'Now there's a question and a half,' he said.

'There's no such thing as half a question,' I said.

He looked at me and the whole room turned grey.

'My wife passed away and we didn't have any children,' he said. 'It wasn't in the big plan, I suppose.'

'What big plan?'

I sat up in the bed.

'We'd have liked kids but it didn't happen,' he said. 'That's all I mean.'

It was unusual having Mr Daly in my bedroom. I looked at him and his grey skin and his grey hair and his grey teeth for approximately five seconds and at the end of that he didn't strike me as horrible anymore. I thought he must hate looking at himself in the mirror and that made him a bit like me.

In a way, he was actually good because when I looked at him I realised things were never going to be the same. He was going to make things different by having sex with my mother and being nice to me.

'I'm thinking about writing a book about this area,' he said. 'All the changes.'

He handed me the pile of photographs. They were all

different sizes.

'Old photographs of around here,' he said.

I looked.

The top one was just a photograph of a rich family from ages ago.

He pointed to a lady in the photograph and said she was the one who was supposed to have drowned in the pond behind Clonduff House. According to the story, she was the ghost, but, he said, the story was actually wrong. It was the body of a little baby that was found in the pond. They never found out who the baby was.

I asked if it was a boy or a girl.

'I don't know yet,' he said. 'I'm looking into it.'

I looked at the blurry face of the woman who was supposed to be the ghost (but wasn't). It was hard to tell if she was happy or sad.

I went on through the pile. They were mainly black and white ones of fields and farmers in the olden days and ones of the pig farm before the pig shed and the caravan. I sort of recognised the farm house.

I wasn't really that interested but I pretended I was. I asked things like where are they and do you know him.

He said where they were or who it was (some of the photos had nobody in them just horses and tractors and fields, the ones with people were mainly the two dead brothers off the pig farm).

If he didn't know who the people were he just said he didn't know.

When we got to the end of the photos he told me that my mother had soup on and I should come down. I said alright and then he just got up and went out and I got out of bed. I went over and put the David Bowie tape on. I pretended I had a microphone in my hand and I did the first song in the mirror like I'd seen Angela do. It wasn't really a song, more a poem. When it was over I took my bow in the mirror.

'I'd like to dedicate that to my friend Angela,' I said.

Everyone went mad cheering.

Then I bent down and looked under the bed and found the story of RottingDead and FlanniganBrannigan. I'd rolled the pieces up and stuck them inside my slippers before I set out to meet Angela the day before. I took the pieces of the story out and put them in the bottom of my wardrobe at the back beside my box of Slenders. Then I put on my clothes and went downstairs.

On the way down I realised that I was starving hungry and also that I loved my mother and had sympathy for her. This was a feeling in my heart but when I actually went into the kitchen she started screaming and shouting at me and the feeling went really quickly and I started screaming and shouting back and it went on from there.

Anyway, that was kind of the end of that part of my life, I suppose.

But it's not like everything got better or anything. For one thing, Angela never turned up again. She was gone, like her sister.

My mother said it would mark our lives forever but, to be honest, I don't think it did.

The gardai came and questioned me and told me that it was very important that I told the truth. But I'd always known that the truth was important. It was everybody else who was telling lies. Not me.

Mr Daly turned out to be a community worker and I needed to have somebody there as well as the gardai when they questioned me, but then when they discovered that he was in love with my mother they got all annoyed and I had to have somebody else in the interview so I was actually interviewed twice.

It didn't matter to me. I just told the truth as I saw it. The papers were full of it. Everybody said that Tony did it, then the father did it, but nobody ever got caught and Marion and Angela never came back.

My mother did a lot of crying. Mr Daly was around a lot. They did a lot of whispering about me. I missed my father and I missed Angela but it was the beginning of me finding out that I was ok with just my own company, that it was better that way.

Things kind of eventually went back to normal i.e. the world became less unusual. I think maybe Angela had made the world unusual, and her being gone made it normal again.

And, funny enough, now that I've written it all down, it seems like it actually happened to somebody else and not to me at all and maybe that's a good thing.

But a couple more things happened that are worth telling about before it's all over and done with. Kind of endings, I suppose.

The first was on Christmas Eve.

It actually snowed and that made everything extra Christmassy. It started after tea and just kept on going and going so there was loads of snow, and it was dark and you could hear your feet crunching it when you went out to the coal shed, and the coal was black and the snow was white, but like in a dream, and all the other colours and sounds in the world were hiding behind this dream.

It was snowing on telly too and we even had special Christmas snow spray on the windows.

Me and my mother were still feeling a bit awkward around each other but a few days had passed since everything had happened and, as I said previously, things were very Christmassy and we both had presents for each other (I'd left her original present in school when I'd legged it so I had to buy her another one, a vase) and we were bound to start talking to each other again because basically we both really liked Christmas.

We even went out into the garden at one stage and looked at the snow falling down out of the dark sky, out of nowhere really, and we tried to catch snowflakes in our mouths.

My mother caught the most and we had a laugh for the first time since everything went wrong and I really liked seeing and hearing her laugh, especially in the snow, especially in the garden.

Afterwards we went in and warmed ourselves at the fire and had toast and tea and I got to thinking about Angela and what she said about being depressed by empty gardens, and it occurred to me that most gardens were empty most of the time anyway and I wondered if it took an already depressed person to think something like that in the first place i.e. that empty gardens are sad.

But anyway, this night Angela wouldn't have been depressed by our garden because me and my mother made good use of it.

Around half eleven we put on our coats and set off for midnight mass. People had candles in their windows and you could see Christmas trees and twinkly lights in houses and everything was quiet and everybody was saying Happy Christmas even though they didn't actually know each other.

Then all of a sudden you could feel something had changed, that everybody was an extra bit excited, even on top of the excited feeling of Christmas Eve and snow, and the people in front of us who were heading for the church changed direction and a couple of them started running, which was hard in the snow, and I heard somebody shouting FIRE! and at that very exact second me and my mother turned the corner onto the main road and you could see orange sparks jumping into the sky over the trees and thick smoke swirling and black in the dark sky.

'Clonduff House must be on fire,' said my mother and, for various reasons, a big shiver ran down my spine.

We crossed the road and through the trees you could actually see flames. The park was all white from the snow and it made the dark seem less dark, sort of glowy, and you could see groups of people standing around with steam coming out of their mouths and hats and gloves on.

I ran right around the trees to the front of the building where the glass patio thing was and, just as I got there, there was the sound of windows smashing and flames and smoke shot out from the upstairs bit, and loads of glass fell on the ground right in front of me.

People were roaring and shouting Get back! Get back! so I walked backwards looking up at the whole top of Clonduff House spewing out huge big orangey flames.

I don't know why but, to be honest, it felt right that it was burning. It felt right that just empty space in the sky would be left where birds could fly through on their way to somewhere else, and they'd never know that Clonduff House had ever been there.

A siren came from far away and got nearer and an extra big flame must have shot up because all of a sudden we were lit up and when I looked around the crowd had got much bigger. People were everywhere and my mother was over talking to Mr Daly and when she saw me looking she started waving her arms around like windscreen wipers.

I was about to wave back and go over to her but then I noticed this weird thing so I didn't, I just stayed where I was, rooted to the spot. I was actually watching this car on the road behind her. It was slipping all over the place. It was funny. It kind of skidded to the side of the road and spun around in slow motion and came to a stop under one of the orange lights.

The snow was thick now, more and more of it coming down, twirling in the wind and landing on everybody and everything.

The door of the car opened and a dog jumped out and started barking at the snow and the sky, and then two people got out behind the dog and there was just something about the dog and the car and the people that kept me watching.

And next of all the dog came running in my direction and one of the people came after him shouting his name and that's when I knew it was Angela's mam and dad, because the dog did know me, because it was Timmy, Angela's dog.

I called him over and he recognised me and started wagging his tail and jumping up and down so I bent down to kiss him, and the crowd seemed to grow even bigger around me and I was looking at loads of legs on all sides and Timmy licking my face and making me laugh. His tongue actually went into my mouth. In the end I had to grab his collar and stand up so he'd stop licking me and when I stood up the crowd was so big I wasn't able to see where I was, just peoples' coats, hats, sleeves etc. so I kind of went back down to Timmy's level and led him out through all the peoples' legs like we were invisible.

I heard a voice shouting Timmy, Timmy! so we headed in that direction and I knew right away that it was Angela's mother who was calling. As we walked toward her I was able to just watch her for approximately seven seconds while she stood there staring at us like she was hypnotised.

You could see her lips moving even though she was saying nothing now and then Timmy yelped and did a kind of dance between us like he wanted us to meet, and I stood up to normal height and then it was like she suddenly came out of her dream world.

I wasn't sure if she knew who I was but she said something anyway although I couldn't hear it because a siren made a big noise just at that second, and a fire engine drove into the park, its blue lights flashing on and off on the snow, and fire men got out and started running around and a garda car arrived too and suddenly people were moving everywhere.

We (i.e. me and Angela's mam) were standing right beside each other now, and I didn't really know what to say, so I just said nothing but she kept shaking her head up and down at me like she was giving signals and then she actually bent down and sort of shouted something in my ear and this is what she shouted:

'Maybe it's a relief for some houses when they burn down.'

I thought it was a weird thing to say and I could smell drink off her so I just smiled and moved my head up and down and went back down on my hunkers to Timmy's level.

When I looked up I could see tears coming out of her eyes so I looked away.

Snow was still falling on top of us, floating down and landing and dissolving and every single flake was completely different and completely the same, and that was more proof of God's existence according to teachers and priests, and somewhere I could hear a boy singing *So here it is, Merry Christmas, Everybody's having fun!* at the top of his voice, and I could actually taste petrol in the air, and there was a huge crack like a big car-ferry splitting in half and sinking to the bottom of the sea, and everybody went O my God! as the roof of the burning house collapsed in on itself and more flames and sparks and black smoke went shooting and swirling into the sky.

I think Timmy got a bit frightened by everything because he started barking and growling and whining at the fire. I gave him a big hug so he wouldn't be scared and he did actually stop barking and everything seemed to go a bit quiet then and I noticed that Pauline, Angela's friend who I didn't like, was standing right there beside us like she'd appeared out of nowhere really. The last time I'd seen her had been at the garda station (she told me that the gardai had made Paul the Rapist cry when they interviewed him).

The situation was unusual because the gardai and Mr Daly had told me to stay away from her, from everybody who knew Angela and Marion.

'Somebody saw the lady in one of the windows,' she said, all excited. 'The roof collapsed on top of her.'

'What lady?' said Angela's mother, and something in the way she spoke made me think that she didn't like Pauline.

'The lady of Clonduff House. The ghost,' said Pauline, looking over as if she wanted me to say something but I kept quiet.

'There's no such thing as ghosts,' said Angela's mother. 'Don't be so foolish.'

Pauline went quiet and just looked at the fire. She looked lonely and lost.

I was wondering whether to tell her what Mr Daly had discovered about the ghost story being wrong because it was a dead baby not a woman in the pond but before I could say anything Mr Daly actually turned up.

'Your mother's after been looking for you everywhere,' he said.

The snow was coming down heavy again and a fireman was telling everyone to push back so the whole crowd was moving and Mr Daly was pointing to where my mother was and I started walking over there but I couldn't find her, and the snow was falling harder, and I thought about ClonduffSiberia for the first time in ages, and how miserable the weather was all the time, except you couldn't really say that snow on Christmas Eve was miserable so, in the end, I didn't think ClonduffSiberia was a good name for that night anyway, and maybe never again.

I was thinking all this and making my way through the blizzard, and things were blurry because the big flames from the fire had sort of died down and funny sounds, rumbles and crackles and big groans and growls, were coming from the house and I could hear Timmy barking somewhere but I was by myself now in a big whirl of blizzard and flashing lights for approximately seven seconds, and the snow froze in the air and the light was blue and white flashes and in the middle of it all, right in front of me, somebody stood there blocking the way, and the somebody was Angela's dad wearing a huge big coat.

We sort of looked at each other and I wasn't sure if he knew who I was but I decided the best thing to do was act like he did so after approximately three seconds I said Happy Christmas and your wife and dog are over there and then I was in the middle of asking him if there was any news about Angela but before I could even finish he was shaking his finger right in my face

'Don't you dare even mention my daughter's name,' he

spat, and his eyes looked like they were going to explode. Time went funny. All the snow was twirling in different direction again and I could smell the burning fires of hell.

'Tell her Happy Christmas if she does come back,' I said.

He actually put his hands over his ears to stop my words going in. He had big, black gloves on. Then he turned and marched away like somebody getting swallowed by a blizzard in the arctic.

'Come on, you.' My mother appeared out of nowhere. 'We'll miss mass altogether if we don't make tracks.'

Her voice sounded like home and I think I needed that just then and so I said ok and we started to walk out of the park, away from everything, back towards the road. We linked arms because the ground was bumpy.

'That family is queer,' she said, and I knew she was talking about Angela's family.

'Were you talking to them?'

'Only to wish the mother well and tell her I was saying a prayer for the girls but, God love her, she's not right.'

She meant right in the head.

'What do you mean?' I said.

'They're selling the house and moving down the country but I'm not sure that's going to solve her problems.'

'What about Angela?' I said. 'Did she tell you anything

about Angela?'

'Nothing that you don't already know. Now let's get moving. We need to say a prayer for that soul of yours.'

The snow was actually stopped now and everything looked lovely and Christmas was here. When we got to the church there was candles everywhere and the wolf-priest was bringing this little plastic doll with glass eyes up to stick it in this big crib they'd built on the altar. You could see the clumps of hair sticking up out of his collar and they were playing tapes of bells and holy music.

The wolf-priest gave the little doll to a little boy or girl who was there specially because it was midnight mass and they put it in the manger, and then everybody sang the hymn, me included, and the wolf-priest smiled at everybody and said Happy Christmas into the microphone like he actually meant it, and then he announced that they'd made enough money to build a proper church made out of bricks and everybody clapped. I'd never heard clapping in a church before.

◆

The other thing that happened was after Christmas.

The telly programmes were back to normal and the new year had started and stuff felt ordinary again.

I was still on my holidays and things were more or less

ok although I was nervous about going back to school because of all the trouble I was in.

But that was still a few days away and me and my mother were getting on well. I'd got my stereo for Christmas and two Bowie records, 'Aladdin Sane' and 'The Man who Sold the World' (my mother later told me that she'd asked Angela what records to get me and she told her those ones) and I was playing them all the time and writing up in my bedroom.

(I'd actually started writing this, i.e. what you're reading now, that is if anybody actually ever does read it, but I wasn't as quick as I expected and it took me until now to finish it. I've mainly been reading books and listening to Bowie in my bedroom and writing and just going to school since all this happened. I miss Angela now and again. Nobody got caught for it, even Tony was found by the police over in England, but they let him go again. It was in all the papers).

Anyway, this Sunday, the first Sunday of the new year, I got on my bike and cycled over to where my father died.

I didn't mean to, it just sort of happened.

The sky was blue with just a few feathery clouds and it was freezing cold. Nobody was out on the streets. I was singing Bowie and I just kept going.

The snow was gone and everything felt sort of cleaner.

Across the park, past Clonduff House, all abandoned

and burnt, (everybody was saying that they were going to build the new church there now but me and Mr Daly were against it) and down into the village, past the Greenlawn Shopping Centre and the library and the credit union, and I just kept going and going and it was as if I knew I was going somewhere but I wasn't sure where and it didn't really matter anyway.

The road he died on was near the block of flats we used to live in before Clonduff so I cycled past that first. I didn't stop though. I just kept going.

It was a big main road but there wasn't much traffic. There was a crossroads halfway down. The tree was there, a big tree, not really growing up straight but sideways and old, and the trunk was so wide that my arms couldn't actually reach around and touch each other. I knew this from the times just after he died when I used to come down here a lot and I really, really wanted to be able to hold that old tree in my arms.

To be honest, nobody had ever pointed out to me the actual spot, the actual tree, but I knew it was this crossroads and somehow I knew as well that it was this tree, this spot. I knew it in my heart, and in my bones.

I stopped my bike and just let it fall on the grassy bit on the side of the road. One of the wheels kept spinning around. Now and then a car whizzed past but it was mainly quiet with the odd bit of wind blowing. There was a scar in the trunk of the tree where the car had smashed into it. I'd seen it before and put my hand into it and thought about the car wrapped around it and the man in the car dying in agony and my father on the side of the road and the bike lying all scrunched up with one wheel going around.

I put my hand into the scar.

I think I was worried that knowing the ghost of the man who died screaming in his car wrapped around this tree, and having spoken to him and everything, that it might make the scar less important.

But it didn't.

It was still the scar made by the car that killed my father. And all of that was still important.

I looked up the tree. It went right up into the sky, like a snake standing up. It didn't have any leaves left on it, just a few bits of plastic blowing in the wind, no birds anywhere, and the branches at the top were sticking out in all directions like as if someone had put a banger in the snake's mouth and its head exploded and then somebody took a picture of that exact second.

The bark was a mixture of colours, and the wind flew through the branches and they swayed a bit and a plane was going across the sky, disappearing behind one branch and then coming out behind another, but never exactly where you'd expect it to be.

I put my arms right around the tree and it creaked like an old hinge. I held on as tight as I could.

A car whizzed past.

It would have looked funny if you were in the car.

Then the car was gone and the road was empty and there was just the wind and I could actually smell the tree.

Acknowledgements

Thanks to everybody who helped, especially Shaun Levin,
Ali Smith, George Maybury, Michael Arditti, Achy Obejas,
Conor MacCabe, Marian Keyes, Darren Walsh, Glenn Phillips
(much missed Gutterheart), Phyllis and Myles, Theresa and Alan,
John O Reilly and Dermod Moore, EB Mazyck-Hill, Margaret
Hurley, Eddy (much missed best boy) Alan Wallis, The Kingsmead
Crew, JMB, Dennis Cooper and the weaklings, David and Ping,
Mike Newton, Andrew Greenhill, Dave, Susannah Riordan, Chris,
Lorraine, and Mia at The National Poetry Library in London,
and Helen, Ray, Aoibhe and Liam in Dublin.

Gratitude to the music of Sinead O'Connor, Damien Dempsey,
The Fall, Kate Bush, Gloria Gaynor and David Bowie

Elements of the story were inspired by the paintings of
Marc Chagall, refugee

Mega-Grats to Mark Paul Ring

Shout out to the O'Loughlin and Behan clans
(also the Rings)

Oh yeah! Love and thanks to Marc Meyer!

Find more Henningham Family Press publications at
henninghamfamilypress.co.uk

All our paperback fiction is reinterpreted in our studio, with the
author, as limited edition handmade Artists' Books.

Subscribers to Henningham Family Press receive all our
paperback fiction at a discount, through their door on publication
day. *Kunstverein* Subscribers receive one handmade limited
edition as well. Find out how to subscribe on our website.

 HENNINGHAM
FAMILY
PRESS